THE CALIBANS

THE PURGATORIUM, BOOK THREE

Eva Pohler

Eva Pohler Books
20011 Park Ranch
San Antonio, Texas 78259
www.evapohler.com

Publisher's Note: This is a work of fiction. Names, characters, places, and incidents are a product of the author's imagination. Locales and public names are sometimes used for atmospheric purposes. Any resemblance to actual people, living or dead, or to businesses, companies, events, institutions, or locales is completely coincidental.

Book Layout ©2017 BookDesignTemplates.com

Book Cover Design by Wydawnictwo Replika

The Calibans/ Eva Pohler. -- 1st ed.
Paperback ISBN: 978-1-958390-53-5

It's all real. Every bit of it, even if it's artistic in some ways and scientific in others, it's all real. It's really happening. That's why it's called living art. You're both a character in a story and someone alive, living an experience.

—CAM

Contents

For my family.

Scorpion Anchorage

Daphne had come all this way, had deceived just about everyone she knew to make it happen, and she couldn't even climb out of the dang boat onto the pier at Scorpion Anchorage.

Her backpack was too heavy. How did she expect to traipse around the entire island with it? Another wave of panic shimmied down her spine, and that voice that had been haunting her since she had made her decision to return repeated its mantra: *You don't know what you're doing.*

A flock of seagulls cried out overhead, as though they were laughing at her.

She frowned at the captain as he handed over her propane canister, which had been stored on the ride over.

Great. One more thing to add to her load.

"I'm gonna have to leave some things here, I guess—if that's okay." She squinted against the bright sun.

He didn't reply, but since he didn't say no, she eased the pack down on a bench, pulled her arms free, and began the frustrating process of deciding which lifesaving items she could live without.

She wasn't going to give up her sleeping bag. She'd rather starve. Her new Jetboil stove was another item she couldn't do without. Plus, it was small—just a two-cup mug that attached to a small propane canister. The beef jerky, oatmeal packs, protein bars, and dried pasta mixes weren't heavy. Should she chuck some of the canned goods? Hmmm. Maybe she really didn't need all these beans and canned chicken.

No. She could imagine Kara shaking a finger: Scaling the bluffs and trudging along in the elements required protein.

The portable phone chargers had to stay. How else would she capture the evidence she needed to bring this place down?

What about her poetry journal? No. She couldn't live without it. It would stay in the pack.

She had bought a tent large enough for two people, because she couldn't stand the coffin-like feeling of a one-person tent. She could probably go without it, but it was the only place where she could ever be sure she wasn't on camera. Her hand circled around the hammer she planned to use to drive in the stakes. It was pretty darn heavy. Maybe she could use rocks instead.

She handed it over to the captain. "You can have this."

He took the hammer without comment as she rummaged around for something else to leave behind.

The captain eyed her jugs of water. "There's fresh water on the campgrounds."

She knew that, but what the captain didn't know was that she wasn't going to be staying on the campgrounds for long.

"The water is your heaviest weight," the captain said. "Dump those, and you'll manage better."

As she was considering the captain's advice, another boat approached the harbor. Daphne nearly shrieked when she saw Dr. Hortense Gray standing among the passengers, holding onto the railing and looking out to shore, like a spider on the edge of its web.

Daphne dropped to her knees and hid behind the side of the catamaran.

The chances of being recognized by Dr. Gray and her staff were pretty slim. Daphne had dyed her hair blonde and was wearing a baseball cap and sunglasses. Her brother Joey's baggy sweatshirt and jeans helped to hide her physique. Besides, no one would be looking for Daphne. No one was expecting her. She blended with the other campers and hikers just fine. But she didn't want to take any chances—especially before she'd even gotten off the boat.

The captain's brows slanted together.

"I don't want to be seen by that woman," Daphne explained. "Please don't give me away. Please?"

"I'm on a tight schedule, miss," the captain said.

All of the other passengers had already gone ashore.

"I'll give you fifty bucks," Daphne said.

His eyes lit up. "Fifty bucks?"

Daphne fished in her back pocket for her wallet, nearly dropping her phone. She pulled out two twenties and a ten and handed them over, considering it money well spent. No way was she going to let this mission be spoiled before it ever began. Too much time, money, and energy had already been put into it.

"Fine." The captain took the cash and returned to his cockpit.

Daphne listened for the other boat to pull away from the pier. Dr. Gray would be circling around to Prisoners Harbor and docking there, which is exactly why Daphne was getting off *here*.

Even Greg didn't know Daphne was returning to the island.

When he'd called her in January, she was at first shocked, then suspicious, and, finally, sympathetic. She had agreed to meet him at a small café one Saturday afternoon, as long as she could bring Brock. It had been a week before Christmas.

Greg was seated at a corner booth when she and Brock walked in. Greg looked thin, nervous, and tired. Dark bags hung beneath his eyes.

"Thanks for coming," he said.

"Glad to see you, man." Brock offered Greg a fist-bump.

"My God." Daphne slid into the booth across from him, unable to peel her eyes away from his gaunt face.

Brock sat next to her. "You don't look so good."

Greg gave them a half smile and shrugged. "No, I guess not."

"How did you get off the island?" Daphne asked.

He had refused to tell her anything over the phone.

"When I found out about Emma…" he stopped for a minute to collect himself.

Daphne bit her lip, feeling awkward. "I never got to tell you how sorry I was for your loss."

"Me, too, man," Brock added.

"So, you know." Greg wiped his eyes, which had filled with tears. "Well, I had no reason to stay. I left, right after you did, I guess. Had to beg for transportation, but I got away."

A waitress asked if she could get them something to drink. They all ordered water.

"What about your mom?" Daphne asked, when the waitress had left.

"Like I said on the phone, I don't want her to know where I am."

"Have you talked to her since you left?" Brock asked.

"No. And you have to promise not to say anything to her."

Daphne was worried about how agitated he'd become. "We promise. We won't say a word."

"You don't have to worry about me," Brock assured him. "I never see her."

"But *you* do," Greg said to Daphne. "She comes to treat your brother. Does she ever talk about me?"

Daphne shook her head. Dr. Gray had come to see Joey twice: once in September and again in November. She was due to return in two weeks. "Whenever I ask how you are, she says you're fine."

Greg laughed, but it wasn't pleasant. The sound from his throat was more a like a cackle. It sounded both evil and heartbreaking.

"I'm sorry," she added, feeling guilty for having allowed herself to forget about the traumas of the Purgatorium. Her brother, Joey, seemed almost like his old self—like before he had accidentally killed their grandfather. Daphne had gone back to school. Her parents were happier. She and Brock were getting along great.

It had been easy to forget.

The waitress returned with their water and asked if they wanted anything to eat. Daphne and Brock ordered the special—chicken-fried steak.

"I don't have any money." Greg looked down at his hands.

"It's on us," Brock said. "Get whatever you want."

Greg thanked them and ordered the special, too.

Daphne peeked over the rail of the catamaran to confirm that the other boat had left. She sighed with relief. It was gone.

"I'm going to be late to my next stop," the captain complained from his cockpit.

Deciding to take his advice, she left the water jugs on the floor of the boat. She had two liters in the bladder of her backpack and lots of iodine tablets for when she got to the stream in Central Valley. She slipped her arms through the straps, hefted the beast onto her back, and climbed onto the pier.

It was time to begin.

With the sun beating down on her from high noon, the shade trees and flat dirt path were a relief as she walked the half- mile trek to her campsite. The park office in Ventura had assigned her to number thirteen. It had been an easy number to remember, because it had been Kara's age when she died.

On the way to her site, Daphne passed two families with younger children, a couple in their twenties, and two groups of men. It was the first Saturday of spring break, so she had expected there would be people, and that was good, because it helped her to blend in.

Her new boots felt comfortable, but the waterproof socks made her hot, and she wanted out of her sweatshirt now that she was off the boat. The wind wasn't nearly as bad here as she remembered it being on the other side of the island. She dropped her pack on a picnic table at a vacant site and stripped off the shirt, having remembered to dress in layers. In fact, she wore a one-piece bathing suit beneath her clothes so she could easily bathe in the stream without stripping down. Then she lathered some sunscreen on her arms. She'd learned her lesson from the last trip.

As she continued on her way, she sipped the water from the tubing that led to the plastic bladder in her pack and thought more about her conversation with Greg at the café back in San Antonio.

"I came here for three reasons," Greg said, once the waitress had left to fill their order. "First, to tell you about Emma. I wasn't sure if you knew."

"We were there when they found her," Daphne said, recalling that night on the beach. The memory of Emma's black and blue body lying on the shore in a heap made her shiver. "I'm so sorry. Do you know what happened?"

Greg sucked in his lips, fighting tears. "We were going to make a run for it during your mom's Limuw ceremony." He took a napkin and patted the beads of sweat forming on his face. "Emma was still recovering from her gunshot wounds. I should have known she wasn't strong enough." He broke down, unable to hold back his sobs.

Brock squeezed Daphne's hand as tears formed in her eyes, too.

"I'm so sorry." She closed her eyes but couldn't shut out the memory of Emma's bruised and broken body.

"She fell from one of the headlands not far from the resort," Greg explained. "I tried to grab her, but I wasn't fast enough. The ocean swallowed her. I swam for hours looking for her, but…"

"Oh my God," Brock muttered.

"I had just given a hiker a note and my last twenty bucks to meet you at Scorpion Anchorage. I don't even know if you ever got that note."

"I did."

"I'm surprised." Greg sipped his water, trying to collect himself. "It was a long shot."

"I tried to get my parents to go back," Daphne said. "I was after them for weeks to get help and go back, but they wouldn't."

"Don't go back there," Greg warned. "Don't ever go back."

She reached her campsite and unburdened the pack onto the picnic table. It didn't take her long to put up the tent and transfer her food into the storage box that came with the site. She hadn't eaten since morning, so she made herself a little lunch with her new Jetboil stove. She boiled two cups of water and added one of the pasta mixes and a can of chicken. She'd eaten this concoction before and knew it was good, but today she couldn't taste the food; she was too nervous.

Once she had finished eating, she washed out the mug to her stove and then went to scope out this part of the island. She stopped first at the Visitor's Center at the historic Scorpion Ranch House—which was nothing like the house at Christy Ranch but was, nevertheless, interesting with its display about the Chumash heritage and the island's plant and wildlife. Then she checked out some of the hiking trails. The open flatlands on this side of the island were easier on her body, but were less scenic. She'd been told by the woman at the Ventura office not to miss the sunset at Potato Harbor, so she followed the trail along the northern shore with a few other hikers and was pleased with the views once she came to the crest overlooking the sea. The spectacular scene uplifted her spirit, but as she headed back toward her tent, tears stung her eyes. That voice of doubt returned, repeating its mantra: *You don't know what you're doing.*

And the simple fact was, she didn't quite know what she was doing. Yes, she had a plan, but it was flimsy at best. Her "Plan A" was to kidnap Cam. She had brought rope, a gag, and chloroform, to help her. If she got caught, she would fall on "Plan B," which was to secretly capture as much video on her phone as possible, something to show the

FBI. In three days, Mrs. Turner would arrive with the police. Mrs. Turner had come with them once before, but Cam had refused to return with his mother, and since he was an adult, there'd been nothing she or the police could do about it; but Daphne didn't turn eighteen for another month. And there was no way, when asked, that she would ever tell the police that she wanted to stay on the island.

Her mind raced back to that afternoon with Greg at the café in San Antonio.

"The second thing I wanted to tell you was…Can you please get your parents to talk to the FBI? What my parents are doing over there, it's criminal. They've got to be stopped."

Daphne arched a brow. "Wait. *Parents? Both* of your parents are over there?"

"Who's your father?" Brock asked.

"Arturo Gomez," Greg answered. "I thought you knew that."

"You introduced yourself as Gregory Gray." Daphne looked back and forth between the two boys. "How could I know?"

So, Greg was Arturo's son. Daphne let that sink in.

"Well, he didn't know about me for the first seven years of my life," Greg explained. "It's a long story. My point is they need to be stopped."

"I've already asked my parents to talk to the police," Daphne said. "They won't. They're too grateful for what your mom has done for me and Joey."

Greg put his face in his hands.

"Why can't *you* go to the FBI?" Brock asked.

"I did—about four years ago. I got handed back over to my parents. No investigation. Nothing but a slap on *my* wrists."

"Why *your* wrists?" Daphne asked.

Greg lifted his brows. "Have you met my mother?"

"What makes you think Daphne's parents can have any better luck?"

"For one thing, they're adults," Greg said. "And for another, they aren't related to her."

"They won't do it. Believe me, I've tried," Daphne said. "If only we had some of the surveillance video, some evidence we could show the authorities."

"What's the third reason?" Brock asked Greg.

Greg bit his lip and squeezed his hands together. "I, uh…"

The waitress brought their plates and a bottle of ketchup. "Get you anything else?"

"No, thanks," Daphne said.

Once the waitress had gone to take the order of another customer, Greg leaned in and said, "I hate to ask this. But my third reason for coming was, well, I was wondering if I could borrow a few hundred dollars." Then he added, "I promise to pay you back."

"Of course," Daphne said, without hesitation.

"Do you have a job?" Brock asked.

"I did," Greg explained. "But if I'm going to have a steady job, I need to change my name, first, and get new identification, so my parents can't find me."

"But your trust fund…" Daphne started.

"You think I want their money? Do you honestly think I want anything to do with my parents?" Greg's eyes widened and he bounced up and down in his seat. "I'd kill myself before I'd take their money."

"Calm down," Brock said. "I get it."

As Daphne reached her tent and crawled inside of that tiny, suffocating space that would be home for the coming days, she felt more alone than ever. She needed to fall asleep so that when darkness came, she could pack everything up and sneak away from the campgrounds to the other side of the island. If she got caught crossing the fence by a park ranger or a conservancy officer, that would be the end of it. No one was allowed on the Nature Conservancy side without a permit. She'd looked into getting one, but she didn't have the training and experience required. Sneaking and breaking the law were her only options.

But if that's what it would take to save her best friend, and maybe all of the Calibans, she would do it. Greg had warned her not to come back to the island without the FBI, but that was before she had spoken to Cam's mom.

It had been early January. Daphne had come home from school. She'd parked in the driveway and was crossing the lawn, when Mrs. Turner appeared beneath the oak tree that divided their two properties.

"Hello, Daphne."

"Oh, hi, Mrs. Turner. How are you?"

Cam's mom folded her arms. "I'm okay, thank you. How about you, dear?"

"Good, thanks."

"By any chance, have you spoken to Cameron recently?"

Daphne shook her head. "Not since we left the island last summer. Why?"

Mrs. Turner's lips trembled. "I don't know how to get in touch with him. He stopped writing to me. He hasn't called, either."

Cam's mom had told Daphne last fall how upset she'd been when she'd learned Cam didn't plan to return to college. He had decided to stay and work for Dr. Gray.

"There's no cell reception there," Daphne said.

"He didn't come home for Thanksgiving or Christmas," A tear slipped down Mrs. Turner's cheek, and she swiped it away with a shaky hand. "I don't know what to do. I'm thinking about going back to the island and bringing him back."

After hours of tossing and turning without a wink of sleep, Daphne put on her headlamp and wrote in her poetry journal. None of the words seemed to flow properly for several minutes, but then she finally caught her rhythm and wrote:

I'm not a girl to be scolded, coddled, or patronized,
Or to be overlooked, tricked, or glamorized.
No Prospero rules me or my fate.
I'm my own island; I forge my own gate
To hell and back.
Call me Caliban, if you like, but this girl will rise
And blight you with her dragon flames and cries
For justice.

She reread the poem, and then, satisfied, put it away and hiked to one of two outhouses on the campground. It was a wooden structure with a non-flushing toilet, bio-degradable toilet paper, and hand sanitizer. The inside walls were covered in writing, worse than any bathroom stall she'd seen at her high school. Much of it was crude and obscene, but a lot of it was declarations of love, like *Lisa loves Richard* and *Jamshid and Marcy forever.* More than love, people seemed to need to declare their existence: *Sam was here, James was here, Jose was here, Paul was here, Trevor was here, Solomon was here, Shirley was here, Juan was here, Cathy was here, Atzimba was here,* and on and on, including *Greg was here.*

She almost fell in the toilet when, in permanent black marker, scrawled on the upper right corner of the door, she read:

Cam loves Daphne.

CHAPTER TWO

A Surprise in the Woods

Daphne returned to her campsite and, with the light from her headlamp, folded up her tent and repacked her backpack, the whole time unable to believe that Cam would have written that. Why couldn't she believe it? He'd told her as much last summer. Didn't he say Daphne would always be his number one? She thought he'd been joking. And maybe he'd been lonely when he scrawled it on the outhouse wall. More likely, it wasn't even the same Cam and the same Daphne, for there was no reason why Cam would have been all the way out here at Scorpion Valley—unless, at some point, he had tried to escape, and in his longing for home, had thought of his best friend.

What if Cam had tried to leave and had been prevented?

A movement by her storage box made her flinch. When she shined her light in the area, an island fox stared back at her. Her heart went wild at the thought that it might be Mini-me, but there was no white device on its tail. The fox was wild and nothing to be worried about. Daphne smiled and said hello.

He must have been waiting for her to open her storage box, because as soon as she did, he snatched one of her protein bars and ran off.

"Well, you have a lot of nerve," she muttered.

Once she was packed, she followed the trail along a ridge overlooking the northern shore. Her wristwatch told her it was a little after nine o'clock. As she trod on, Daphne thought more about the last time she had spoken with Cam's mom.

"My letters to Dr. Gray are still unanswered," Mrs. Turner said one afternoon, in the middle of February, while they were alone on Daphne's front porch.

A feeling of nausea overcame Daphne. "Are you worried?"

"Aren't you?"

Daphne nodded.

"When the police wouldn't help me…"

"Why wouldn't they?"

"An officer went down there with me, to the resort, but Cameron refused to leave. He's an adult, and so there was nothing the officer could do."

"I'm so sorry." Tears pricked Daphne's eyes.

"And your parents, well, they sing Dr. Gray's praises and seem unconcerned about Cameron. They keep saying he wants to be there, that he's helping people, and that I should be proud of him."

"I know." Daphne shuddered at how easily her parents could forget the torment they went through on the island, but she had to admit that her feelings for Dr. Gray were mixed. Daphne was grateful that the therapy had helped her and the members of her family from their survivor's guilt and post-traumatic stress disorder. Daphne's episodes of PTSD were now few and far between.

"I'm so sorry I ever told them about that place," Mrs. Turner added.

Daphne supposed she was *not* sorry. In fact, Daphne was *glad* she'd been there.

"So I hired what they call a de-programmer," Mrs. Turner continued. "I paid him quite a lot of money to go to the island, find Cameron, abduct him, and bring him back so we could talk some sense into him. But it's been over a month, and I've heard nothing."

"Over a month?"

"You probably heard that my husband and I have separated."

Daphne hadn't. "No. I'm so sorry." Mrs. Turner was referring to Cam's stepdad, who'd been more like Cam's real father than his biological father ever had. "And he won't help you, for Cam's sake?"

Mrs. Turner shook her head. "And Cam's father won't listen to me. He thinks I'm overreacting. Of course, the real reason he won't help is that he's too busy with his new life, new wife, and new kids. He doesn't care about Cameron."

Daphne didn't know what to say to that.

"I have no choice but to go myself…"

"No," Daphne interrupted, unable to fathom the thin, frail woman navigating the challenges of the island and the psychological antics of the resort. "I'll go. But you have to help me."

She had wanted to ask Brock to come but had been afraid he'd try to talk her out of it. Brock might have told her parents, too, and then her plans with Cam's mom would have been ruined. Now, as she reached the crest of Scorpion Canyon, she stared out over the endless waters and the endless sky and wished he was with her, holding her hand.

And yet, she had to give herself credit, she thought, as she wiped her eyes and refused to cry. The last time she had come to this island, she had come ready to surrender to the grief and injustice of the world. She had come to die. But this time, she was ready to fight, not just for her own life, but for the lives of Cam and Giovanni and the others.

With her dragon flames, she reminded herself.

She followed the canyon ridge inland, away from the northern shore. According to the map, this trail would take her the ten miles all the way to Prisoners Harbor, where she would cross out of the national park and onto the conservancy. The night was clear, and the stars were bright, so once she was out of the small grove of trees, she decided to turn off the headlamp, just in case anyone else was out and about tonight.

Eventually the dirt trail became a gravel road. As she topped a hill and began her descent, she recognized where she was: she was below the naval tower, where she and Brock had once ran from two naval guards. This meant the woods on the other side of the road were travelled by Hortense's lot. In fact, in those very trees had been a speaker system and probably even surveillance cameras. She knew this because when she and Brock had rested beneath those trees, she'd heard her name whispered, just before the Calibans had come dressed as ghosts to frighten and herd her. At the time, she hadn't known Brock was in on the games.

He had been trying to help, she reminded herself. Dr. Gray was to blame, not Brock. Not her parents. Even the Calibans weren't at fault. They'd all been brainwashed by the doctor and her team—Mary Ellen Rose and Lee Reynolds.

What if the doctors had been brainwashed, too? What if they were also victims of some psychological mumbo jumbo they had come to believe in? After all, their methods did seem to work. Daphne recalled the articles she had read about Hortense's adoptive father and the scars all along Hortense's arms.

What about free will? Weren't they all free individuals with the ability to make choices about what they would and would not do? Wasn't Cam free to choose to be here, even if his mother didn't like it?

No. Dr. Gray's methods were psychologically manipulative. She put her victims into a state of terror and helplessness. Daphne had done some research on brainwashing before coming back to the island. She'd read that often people who were brainwashed suffered from what was called the Stockholm syndrome, named after a bank robbery in Stockholm, Sweden where the hostages fell in love with their abductors and defended them in court. According to her research, prisoners of war and victims of domestic abuse sometimes came to feel affection for their abusers, because the victims would become grateful for the slightest kindness shown to them by their abusers. Daphne read that this syndrome was likely an evolutionary adaptation that helped humans as a species to survive.

Dr. Gray had terrified Daphne and her family, and then, in having Daphne choose between the bucket and the rose, she'd made Daphne feel grateful and appreciative and relieved. It was almost impossible not to choose the rose.

So it wasn't really a choice. It was a manipulation. Maybe no one ever chose the bucket—or only a very few, rare individuals.

And then by having the rest of the group watch the victims present the doctors with the rose, Dr. Gray promoted the idea to the others that her methods were right and good.

But were they? Daphne and her family were undoubtedly better off.

Daphne shrugged off those thoughts, reminding herself that she was here to rescue Cam and maybe get some evidence. She'd let the FBI decide whether the doctors' methods were justified.

The road turned into a steep incline, and she climbed up the ridge, which was now above the treetops. She could just make out the naval tower in the distance, its dark silhouette stark against the moonlit night. From here, she could also see Mount Diablo far to the northwest and Sierra Blanca far to the southwest. Between them and invisible to her was Central Valley. And just south of Central Valley and east of Sierra Blanca was the resort.

Her teeth made a little chatter. She hoped she knew what she was doing.

As she stopped at the top of the hill to catch her breath, she heard a sound on the gravel a few feet away. She clicked on her headlamp, thinking it might be a snake. She gasped at the sight of a jean-clad pair of legs curled to one side. She followed the legs to the trunk, crossed arms, shoulders, and face, the eyes, which squinted in her headlamp.

She knew that face.

"Giovanni?"

He scrambled off the edge of the road and into the woods.

"Wait!" She dropped her backpack and ran after him. "Giovanni! It's me! Daphne!"

She stopped and listened for him, unable to find him with her light. She heard him panting in the shrubs a few feet away. Realizing she'd frightened him, she backed away.

"I didn't mean to scare you. What are you doing out here? Are you okay?"

"Why should I trust you?" he asked from his hiding place.

"I don't know." She wasn't even sure if *she* should trust *him*.

"Why didn't you bring the FBI?"

"My parents wouldn't let me. And Cam's mom couldn't even get the police to help." She hoped she wasn't giving herself away. But no one knew she was coming. Dr. Gray couldn't possibly have sent Giovanni out this way to meet her on the road, could she?

Giovanni crawled from the shrubs. His hair was shorter than it had been the last time she had seen him. He must have had his Limuw ceremony a few months ago. Dark rings surrounded his eyes, and he was thin—much thinner than she recalled. He was also covered in white dirt from the gravelly road.

"What are you doing way out here?" Daphne asked again.

"What are *you* doing here?" he asked.

"I came back to rescue Cam for his mom." God, she hoped she hadn't just made a mistake. What if he was wearing a surveillance device? "Now, tell me the truth."

He climbed to his feet. "What do you think? I'm trying to get off the island."

"But it's been nine months. Have you…"

"I was brainwashed, just like Cam and the rest of them—a total puppet. And then about a week ago, I woke up."

"Why?"

"I saw something."

"What?"

"How do I know they didn't send you to find me?"

"How do *I* know they didn't send *you* to find *me?*" she said.

He pointed to the delicate silver chain around her wrist. "You're still wearing your bracelet."

It was true. As much as she hated this place, she loved what the bracelet represented—the old psychological bondage being replaced by the bonds of family and friendship.

She glanced at his wrist. "Where's yours?"

"I threw it into the sea. I have no family or friends."

"I'm your friend."

He looked her up and down. "If that's true, can I have some of your food and water?"

She went back to where she had dropped her pack and called him over, holding the tubing out for him to drink. He sucked on it like he'd been without fresh water for quite some time.

Then she pulled out a protein bar and gave it to him. "How long have you been hiding out here?"

"Thanks." He ripped open the wrapper and gulped it down. "Three days, I think."

She gave him another one. "Let's set up camp in these woods, and I'll make you a warm meal."

These weren't the woods where the Calibans had herded her and Brock, but that didn't mean they didn't have cameras. Daphne found a flat spot and made her camp, even though this would mean she would have to wait to cross the fence tomorrow night and lose a day of work.

After Giovanni had eaten and Daphne had washed out the mug to the stove and had plugged her phone into her portable charger, she spread out her sleeping bag and the two of them lay down with their backs to one another. She had so many questions, but she could tell he was exhausted. And now that she was no longer alone, she felt less frightened. Something told her she could trust Giovanni, even though she wouldn't allow herself to trust him completely. For now, she would take comfort in the presence of a friend—an ally, who would make this situation slightly less terrifying for the moment. She closed her eyes and went to sleep.

CHAPTER THREE

Giovanni's Warning

Daphne awoke to the sound of sobbing. Giovanni was crying in his sleep. Not sure whether she should wake him or let him work through whatever nightmare he was dreaming, she watched his face twist in agony. His usually round eyes and dark brows were pinched together. His dimples were only visible when he grimaced. His mouth and thin lips twitched, opened, closed, and grimaced, as though he wanted to speak.

For a moment, he looked like Joey.

When she couldn't take it anymore, she jostled his foot.

"Huh?" He opened his eyes and looked around.

"You were dreaming."

He wiped his eyes. "Oh."

"You okay?"

He cleared his throat and sat up. "I don't know why I bother."

"With what?"

"Never mind."

She got out her stove and filled the mug with water. "Do you like oatmeal?"

"Yeah. Sure."

They sat with their legs crossed, facing each other and waiting for the water to boil. It only took a few minutes. Then she added a pack of oatmeal mix to the mug and stirred it with her spork.

She handed the mug to Giovanni. "You go ahead. I'll make another batch for me when you're done."

"Wow. Thanks." He blew on each bite before spooning it into his mouth. "It's good. Amazing, actually. I owe you."

"You can repay me by telling me what happened after I left last summer."

Giovanni took another few bites of the oatmeal, and just when Daphne thought he was going to ignore her, he said, "I gave them the rose. But I really wasn't sure what my choice would be, up until the very end."

She nodded. "Same with me."

"They made me feel like I was a part of something," he continued. "Made me feel like I belonged. Like I had a purpose."

"What changed?"

He scraped the last of the oatmeal into his mouth. When he'd finished, he handed the mug and spork over. "Thanks."

She reached her hands through the tent and rinsed out the mug before refilling it.

"I found out what happens to the ones who give the doctors the bucket," he finally said.

She furrowed her brows. So there *were* people who chose the bucket. Did this mean Daphne was a weak person, to have given into the psychological manipulation, where others could hold their own against it? After everything that she'd been put through—the elevator, the cave, the shark attack, the horse-bucking, the ghosts at Christy Ranch, and Stan and Brock's betrayal—after all she had endured with Emma getting shot and the helicopter nearly killing Daphne and her father—even though she and her parents had struggled to escape after Greg's warning, Daphne had still given the three doctors the rose.

Why? Because they had made her want to live again. They had helped Joey come back from wherever he had gone to check out on life. They had brought her parents back. It was like Hortense Gray had said: she had resurrected Daphne and her family from the dead.

Except for Kara. Some things were immutable.

Daphne had been grateful, but not for *a slight kindness*, like the victims of the Stockholm syndrome; the doctors had cured Daphne and had made her brother and parents better, too.

Giovanni wrapped his knees in his arms, like he was hugging himself. "Emma gave them the bucket. Did you know that?"

She shook her head.

"That's why Dr. Gray was trying to keep her and Greg apart."

"I don't understand."

"The ones who give the doctors the bucket are considered beyond saving."

"Just because they don't agree with the methods…"

"I know. But these doctors think they're gods."

"What makes you say that?" She ripped open a package of oatmeal and added it to her boiling water. "Did Dr. Gray call herself Prospero to you, too?"

"Like I said. I saw something."

She took a bite of the oatmeal, waiting for him to explain, not wanting to seem pushy.

"It's so weird how you can totally believe in something," Giovanni said, "and then something will happen to make you realize it was all a lie. It's hard to face the truth, though. It's easier to believe the lie. Waking up hurts."

"You said you saw something."

"A guy—a girl actually, about your age, maybe older, arrived around three weeks ago." He hugged his knees more tightly and rocked himself back and forth. "Her name's Toni, and she says she's a girl trapped in a boy's body, and no one understands her, and she's really angry at the world and everyone in it."

"Kind of like you?"

"I'm not so much angry as indifferent," he said with a sniff. "I guess I was angry when I was younger, but now, I'm like, whatever."

"What about your new family—the one that sent you here? I thought they'd adopted you?"

"Not yet. They were in the process, and I may have blown it with them."

"Why would you say that?" She scraped up the last of her oatmeal.

"After my Limuw ceremony, I wanted to stay and help the others, but my foster parents were shocked by everything and didn't understand. They wanted off the island fast."

Daphne recalled the way her own parents had wanted off, right after the ghosts had paid them a visit. "Did Dr. Gray put them through exercises?"

"Not as bad as what she put yours through. I guess she didn't feel like they needed the therapy."

"So, what happened?" Daphne rinsed out her mug and dried it with her towel.

"I refused to go home with them."

"Oh, no. Are you serious?"

He closed his eyes and nodded.

"I'm sure they'd take you back, now that you've changed your mind."

"I don't know. They were pretty hurt."

"You didn't mean to hurt them."

Tears flooded Giovanni's eyes. "Exactly. I got caught up in, in, this stupid place."

"You aren't the only one. It's like Dr. Gray is a hypnotist."

"If I only knew *then* what I know now."

"And what exactly is that, Giovanni?"

He leaned back on his hands. "I saw the three doctors talking."

"What did they say?" She leaned forward.

"They were in that surveillance room. You've seen it, right?"

She nodded.

"I'd gone to Dr. Gray's office to tell her something. See, she'd offered to adopt me." His eyes filled with fresh tears. "And I was going to tell her I was ready."

"Oh, wow." Poor Giovanni. He must have really been brainwashed to want Dr. Gray for a mother. Then Daphne recalled that Emma had considered the doctor her mother, too.

Giovanni shifted from one hand to another. "But she wasn't in her office. Then I heard the voices coming from that surveillance room. I didn't want to interrupt, so I waited. I could see them through the crack in the door. Mary Ellen Rose was yelling at Hortense Gray."

"What was she saying?"

"They were arguing about science and art and watchers."

"What about them?" Daphne recalled what Hairy Larry had once said about the watchers, and about living art.

"Well, Lee Reynolds said something about it not being art anymore, but entertainment for money. And Hortense was saying the entertainment was therapy, too."

"You're not making any sense. What does that all mean?"

"Just listen."

She waited for him to go on.

"So then Hortense Gray said they'd already sold their souls to the devil a long time ago."

"What?"

"And Mary Ellen said she thought they weren't going to do anymore grand finales."

"Grand finales?"

Giovanni's face turned pale as he said, "Emma was a grand finale."

"What does that even mean? Greg said…"

"And they are planning to create a grand finale for Toni, because the watchers expect it."

"Are you saying they plan to…"

"Drive him—her—to jump."

Daphne's eyes grew wide. "But Emma didn't jump."

"How do you know?"

"Greg…"

"You can't believe him."

"But…"

"Listen to me, Daphne. Greg is one of them. He is his mommy and daddy's right-hand man. He left for a while. I thought maybe he had run away. But he's back now, and he's helping with the games."

"He came to me for help over two months ago." Daphne felt suddenly faint and dizzy. She had believed Greg and had even loaned him three hundred dollars.

"Maybe to get you back here."

"But why?" She searched Giovanni's face for answers. Was he really telling her the truth, or was *he* the one pulling her into another exercise? Her fingers trembled in her lap, because now she realized she had to choose between believing Greg and believing Giovanni. One of them was lying to her.

"Because it's how they make so much money. They keep people coming back, and the doctors either brainwash them into their lapdogs, or torment them for the entertainment of the watchers. The watchers are the investors. They subscribe to a private channel and watch the games, and sometimes even enter them, for entertainment. Dr. Gray says it's therapy for them, too, but I don't think she likes that she has to please them. I think she resents them but sees them as a necessary evil."

Daphne shook her head. This was too much. "What about Cam? Is he still a lapdog?"

"More than ever."

"Did he ever try to run away, like Greg?"

"They left together, but Cam never made it off the island." Giovanni shrugged. "I could never tell if he had gone to spy on Greg, or if he was really trying to escape."

"But now he's helping with the exercises again?"

"Yes, and we have to get out of here as soon as possible," Giovanni said. "Before something happens to Toni. We have to get help."

"No one will help us."

"When the FBI hears what I told you…"

"Why should they believe you? Do you have proof?"

Giovanni shook his head.

"We have to get proof. It's the only way." Daphne decided she would move forward with her plan—whether Giovanni was lying or not didn't change her mission.

Giovanni hugged his knees more tightly to his chest. "There's no way I'm going back to that side of the island."

She'd rather have him with her, even if he was meant to pull her back into the games. "But we have to. We have no choice."

CHAPTER FOUR

A New Friend at Camp Del Norte

Daphne and Giovanni folded up the tent and packed everything up in the backpack.

"So have you decided?" Daphne asked him. "Are you coming with me, or going on your own?"

Giovanni sighed. "I've come a long way to Scorpion Anchorage to turn back now."

"If you really want to help Toni…"

"I've got to look out for me, too, you know. I might have starved to death if you hadn't come along. Seriously." Tears welled in his red-rimmed eyes.

Daphne realized at that moment that Giovanni had always had to watch out for himself, first and foremost. It's why he left her in his dust when Phil frightened them in that Big Foot costume in Central Valley last summer. Giovanni had never had anyone to look out for him, so he hadn't learned how to look out for others.

He stood there on the verge of tears, a frightened boy alone in the world.

Daphne had always had parents who loved her, even when she thought she didn't.

"If you want to go back to the mainland, I totally understand," she finally said. "But where will you go? Back to your foster parents?"

She didn't have enough food for the both of them, anyway.

"I guess so. I'll call them when I get to Ventura, and, I mean, hopefully they'll come get me."

"So you've decided, then?"

"I'm sorry, Daphne," he said. "I'll do what I can to get help over here, okay?"

She nodded, butterflies suddenly flapping in her stomach at the thought of being alone again. "Okay. But don't get my parents involved. I don't want them to know I'm here, and I certainly don't want them on this island ever again."

"I don't even know where they live or how to contact them."

"All right then."

"Thanks for everything." He hugged her. "Good luck."

"Same to you." She handed him a folded piece of paper she had torn from her poetry journal earlier, in case he did decide to leave. "My phone number. Stay in touch, okay?"

"You bet."

"See ya."

He turned to go but then stopped to face her one more time. "Hey, you might not remember this, but the first time I met you, you told me something that changed my life."

She couldn't imagine that she really had that kind of power—to change someone's life—nor could she think what it was she had said.

"I told you that I didn't have a single person in my life that was devoted to my well-being, and you said that maybe *I* needed to be that person."

She nodded, remembering.

"I've decided to do that. Thanks."

She watched him follow the road in the direction she had just come from, hoping deep in her gut that he wouldn't turn around and circle back to the resort to tell the others her plans. She watched until he disappeared down the hill. Then she strapped on her pack and trod on.

After hiking along the navy road for over two hours, she came upon the Del Norte Trail and took it to the backcountry campground. Unlike Scorpion Valley, this area had no proper campsites, fresh water, or toilet. The nearest restroom was about a half-mile trek up to Prisoners Harbor. Glad to have finally made it to the place that would serve as her home base, Daphne wiped the sweat from her brow and scouted for a spot to put her tent among, but not too close to, the three already erected there.

"Well, g'day, Gorgeous," a guy with an Australian accent said from behind her.

She turned to see a tall, thin, bearded brunette with sea-green eyes smiling at her. He looked to be in his early twenties.

Blushing, and not sure if she was flattered or creeped out, she pushed her sunglasses back up on her nose and said, "Hello."

"Want some help setting up?" he offered.

"No, thanks. I've got it."

He pointed to a flat area just behind his tent. "There's an ant mound there, so watch yourself."

"Thanks."

"I pitched there last night and found myself covered in the bities this morning."

"Ouch. That doesn't sound fun."

"Nope. Not one bit." He stretched out a hand for a shake. "I'm Bill."

She took his hand. "D-Darla." *Better safe than sorry*, she thought. She doubted the Australian was connected with the resort—though there was always that possibly—but someone else might overhear.

"Nice to meet you, Darla."

"Likewise."

She found a spot about ten feet away from the others and began setting up. The Australian must have taken the hint that she wanted to be left alone, because he went back to washing his breakfast dishes in a tub just outside his tent. Once she'd situated her things inside her own, she looked at her watch. It was ten in the morning. If she waited to cross the fence line at night, she'd have to waste an entire day.

She returned to the Australian's campsite. "Excuse me, Bill?"

"Yeah?"

"I, uh, seem to have lost my permit and was wondering…how strict are the conservancy officers about checking for them?"

"Oh, the greenies are sticklers," he said. "They have a post at the gate just past Prisoners Harbor. They stop everyone, I believe. Even on Sundays."

"Great." She folded her arms, wondering how Dr. Gray's jeeps were able to get from Prisoners Harbor to the resort without passing through a gate. "Okay, thanks."

"They'll let you in if you're with a guide, as long as the guide has a permit."

What was he getting at?

He gave her a wink. "If you need me, I'm happy to oblige."

"So you're familiar with this island?"

"Not this one. I've been twice to Anacapa—once last summer and again in February. Winter is the best time for that one. Enormous cliffs and these gorgeous yellow flowers that only bloom in cold months. Bloody ace."

"I didn't know that."

"Santa Rosa is my favorite island, though. I just came from there. My third trip. The Chumash ruins and archaeological sites are incredible, not to mention the endemic wildlife."

"So, what brought you to Santa Cruz?"

"I'm gradually making my way around all the Channel Islands. I've also just been to San Miguel and Santa Barbara, so this is my last stop on this trip, though I'm sure I'll be back in the summer."

"Where are you from originally?"

"I grew up in Australia. I've been travelling abroad ever since my parents died two years ago."

"Oh. I'm sorry about your parents."

"Yeah, me too. Anyway, if you want to tag along with me, you're welcome."

She gave him a smile. "Thanks. I'll let you know."

She decided to walk up to the toilet at Prisoners Harbor and think about her options. She could go with her original plan and wait to cross at night, when the gate was closed but unmanned. Or she could go south of the fence to the coastline, which would put her near the big, sprawling oak tree. The fence didn't reach that far, but if she went in that direction, she'd have to scale all those bluffs to get to the resort, and she'd have to enter from the beach, which was under surveillance. If she crossed at the gate, she could easily follow the road into Central Valley, get her much needed water from the stream, and then slip into the compound from a number of directions.

As she neared Prisoners Harbor, she kept an eye out for people from the resort. She doubted anyone would be able to recognize her in her baseball cap, blonde hair, and sunglasses, but that didn't mean she shouldn't be careful.

Sure enough, when she crossed the kayak rental to visit the outhouse, she spotted Hairy Larry talking to a group of four. They each wore lifejackets and had a kayak, and since they were dry, she suspected they were just getting started. Her heart nearly skipped a beat when she noticed Cam among them. She ducked down and rushed into the outhouse.

The toilet was stinky, but Daphne held her breath and tried to gather her thoughts. She needed to pull herself together if she was to have any chance of saving Cam. Maybe she should take Bill up on his offer. She doubted anyone from the resort would be suspicious of an Australian and a blonde American hiking around the conservancy together.

When she returned to her campsite, she found Bill in front of his tent loading a pack on his back.

"I'm headed to the west side of the island to check out the Chumash ruins," he said. "You're welcome to tag along, but, just so you know, it's a far hike, I'm talking back of Bourke—which, in Australia means a hell of a long way—and I won't likely return here until nightfall."

"I could always return earlier on my own, couldn't I?"

"As long as no one catches you without your permit."

"Do you think the conservancy officers scout around the island?"

"I dunno."

With most of her things unloaded, her pack was much lighter. She zipped up her tent to protect her food from wildlife and then set off with Bill toward the gate.

It was hot and muggy down in the shallow valley of the camping area, but when they topped the hill toward Prisoners Harbor, the wind quickly cooled them off. They took a trail away from the shore, so there was no chance of seeing Cam and Larry with their kayak group, thank goodness. The fence came into view, and Daphne was surprised that it wasn't much—just a chain link fence, easy to climb. It also disappeared into the landscape, making it hard to spot in places. The road Roger always took from Prisoners Harbor ran along the canyon ridge, high above, which explained why she had not noticed the fence before.

The man at the gate checked Bill's permit.

"She's with me." Bill jabbed a thumb toward Daphne.

"Ah. She has one of them bracelets. She's allowed through anyway."

Daphne gasped. "My bracelet? Why?"

"Aren't you one of Arturo Gomez's guests?" the man asked.

Daphne nodded as blood rushed to her cheeks. She glanced around for surveillance cameras but spotted none.

"He gives all his guests those bracelets, so we know to leave them alone."

"Who's Arturo Gomez?" Bill asked.

"He practically owns this side of the island," the man said. "He provides the majority of the nature conservancy's funding."

Daphne and Bill passed through the gate and continued along the trail.

"Looks like you didn't need me after all," the Australian said.

"I guess not."

"So, what does it mean to be a guest of Gomez's, anyway?"

"He runs a resort just south of here, hidden in a canyon."

"A resort? On the island? I had no idea."

"It's not on any of the maps. It's very private."

"Well, ain't you lucky?"

Daphne grimaced.

"Why the long face? You didn't care for it?"

They came around the bend that overlooked Central Valley. In spite of everything that had happened there, it met her with magnificent beauty—grassy knolls, purple mountain glory, and a glistening stream. Mount Diablo towered over them to their right and Sierra Blanca to their left.

Bill must have noticed her expression. "Now that's a corker of a view, ain't it?"

"Breathtaking."

"Yet you didn't care for the resort?"

She snapped from her reverie. "The buildings and amenities were amazing, but the staff was not what you'd expect."

"It's got running water, electricity, and the whole nine yards?"

"It's a modern resort. Everything but wi-fi and cell reception."

"If it's not too far, I'd love to see it."

"I'm not sure they welcome trespassers."

"Why aren't you staying there now?"

"It's kind of cultish." As soon as she had said it, heat rushed to her face. Had she just made a huge mistake? Or could she trust the Australian?

"Cultish?"

Daphne swallowed hard. She needed a friend right now and wanted to take the chance that he wouldn't think she was crazy. "It's actually a private rehabilitation facility for people with depression."

He whistled. "Sounds exy."

"Exy?"

"Expensive. And this is a beautiful place for that sort of thing."

"It's a beautiful resort, but it's pretty scary, too. Everyone there is brainwashed."

"What do you mean?"

"It's run by a group of psychologists."

"So?"

Her heart skipped a beat. Was she making a mistake in talking to him? "They believe in scaring the crap out of people to make them appreciate life."

"That's different."

"They go too far. A girl *died* last summer." Her heart pounded against her ribs. She hoped she was making the right decision in trusting the Australian.

"Seriously?"

She nodded.

"And she wasn't the first casualty, either. I've come back to rescue my best friend. He's spellbound by the doctors. His mom is scared to death for him."

"Rescue? How do you plan to do that?"

"I'm still figuring that out. I need to look around first and find the right opportunity to get him to come with me." She began her descent into the valley, and Bill followed. "But first I need drinking water and a bath."

<u>CHAPTER FIVE</u>

A Close Call in Central Valley

As they made their way down a dirt road to the cluster of trees—where, on her first day on the island, Daphne had witnessed the supposed abduction of a girl—Daphne and Bill shared information about themselves. The Australian was easy to talk to. He'd graduated from a university with a history degree and, after his parents had died, he'd put off going to grad school to travel the world. He wasn't sure what he wanted to do or where he wanted to live, so he'd been a nomad for the past two years. He'd mostly travelled the west coast of North America, up as north as Canada and as south as Mexico, but the Channel Islands were his favorite discovery.

"Do you have any brothers or sisters?" Daphne asked.

"Four older brothers. Two live in California, one in England, and the other in Sydney. What about you?"

She should have known he would ask the question back, but even after all her healing here on the island, she still found it difficult to explain to people that her sister had died, and her brother was struggling with mental illness. She made herself do it, though. She started from the beginning, from that day Joey had accidentally killed their grandfather to the night Daphne had heard the banging of Kara's headboard against the wall between their bedrooms. She told Bill the entire story, including her attempted suicide and her parents' decision to send her to the island. She wasn't sure why she was telling him all the details, but she was surprised how saying them all made her feel lighter. And Bill was a good listener.

Before they reached the stream, Daphne warned Bill about the surveillance cameras around the island.

"No kidding?" he asked, furling his brows.

"I know it sounds crazy. You don't have to believe me. Just don't mention anything about my plans again, okay? Not unless I bring them up."

He gave her a nod, but she could tell he wasn't too sure about her.

She knelt at the stream and removed the bladder from her backpack to fill it with water. Then she added the iodine.

"It's probably fresh," Bill said. He knelt down and scooped some to his mouth. "Mmm. Bloody ace. Give it a burl."

She'd tasted it before, but she didn't want to risk it again. "Better safe than sorry," she said. "The last thing I need is to get sick while I'm here."

"Yeah. I understand." He scooped up more onto his face. "This sure feels nice."

"I wouldn't mind taking a quick dip," Daphne said. She felt sticky and stinky.

"You don't mean in the nuddy, do you?"

"What does that mean?"

"I mean, you don't intend to strip all the way down to your birthday suit?"

She blushed and showed him the strap of her yellow one-piece.

"Ah. You wore your cozzie. Mine's back at the tent. Would you be offended if I stripped down to my grundies?"

She blushed again. "No. Of course not."

They dropped their packs and stepped out of their clothes. She dug a bottle of shampoo from her bag and dipped a toe into the stream.

"It's cold!" she said.

Careful not to remove her sunglasses, in case cameras were pointing at her, she waded out to her waist and then sank down on her knees, submerging to her shoulders. "Oh my gosh!" she cried, trying to get used to it. More than a chill scurried down her spine when she realized she was sitting in the very spot where she had tried to drown herself last summer.

"Bloody cold!" Bill echoed as he stumbled in beside her in a pair of white briefs.

"I'm gonna wash my hair real quick," she said, without looking at him. "You're welcome to borrow some of my shampoo."

"If you don't mind."

She poured some of it into his hand and then gave herself some.

"Thanks heaps," he said, dipping his head back and then lathering in the shampoo.

"No problem," she said, as she did the same.

"Oh, this is nice. I haven't washed my hair in a week."

Daphne laughed. She could barely stand to go two days.

Just as she finished rinsing, she heard the sound of horses and human voices coming into the valley. Her heart pounded in her chest when she recognized Kelly leading a group of trail riders directly toward her and Bill.

"Oh, no." Daphne was suddenly seized with fear. This would ruin everything.

Bill glanced at the riders. "What's wrong?"

She pointed at the group coming down the hill.

"You're shaking like a leaf. Are they with…"

"Yes."

"No worries. I'll give the mob a flick."

"What?" She had no idea what he was saying, and the riders were nearly up beside the stream, maybe twenty yards away.

He stepped in front of her, positioning himself between Daphne and the approaching group.

She moved up against his back, trembling uncontrollably.

"No worries, dear," he said kindly.

She slipped her arms around his waist and buried her face in his back.

"G'day," Bill said when the group came to a stop nearby.

"Oh, hello there," Kelly said. "Sorry to intrude."

"No worries. My wife and I were just having a bath. Do you think you could move your party downstream?"

"Of course."

Daphne peeked over Bill's shoulder and gasped. Kelly, Philip, and Mary Ellen were joined by Stan, Bridget, and a girl Daphne didn't recognize."

"Follow me," Kelly said.

"You doing okay, Lisa?" Stan asked.

"Yes," the new girl said.

Was Lisa the newest patient?

Once the riders were out of sight, Daphne let go of Bill.

He turned and wrapped his arms around her. "I'm sorry, mate. You're okay now, ain't ya?"

She wiped her eyes and nodded.

He released her and took the small bottle of shampoo from her shaking hand.

"They're gone. Relax. You're scaring me."

"I'm sorry."

"No need to apologize. Let's get out of this cold water and onto dry land."

He took her hand and led her back to the bank.

"Have you got a towel?"

"In my pack." She tried to unzip her backpack, but her hands were still trembling uncontrollably.

"You poor thing. Let me help you."

Once he got her bag open, she found a clean towel and covered her face—without removing her sunglasses.

"I'm sorry," she said again.

He pulled a rag from his pack and dabbed himself. "No apology necessary, Darla. But I think you might be in over your head."

He was right. Just seeing them all again had her falling to pieces. Exactly how was she going to save Cam?

Still trembling, Daphne climbed into a clean pair of shorts before slipping on her socks and boots. Enough stalling. She'd gotten her water and her bath. It was time to act.

"You go on to the ruins without me," she said to the Australian.

"I can't just abandon you in the face of danger," Bill objected as he climbed into his trousers. "Not after everything you've told me."

"How do you know I'm not a nut case?" She slid on her pack, regretting that she had confided in him. "I could be making it all up."

"I want to see this place."

"Well, if you get caught, don't say I didn't warn you." She headed up the hill toward the resort.

Bill quickly tied his boots and followed. "I can look after myself, thanks."

Daphne stopped in her tracks as an idea came to her. "Wait a minute."

He caught up to her. "What's wrong?"

"Do you really want to help me?" she whispered.

"What do you have in mind?"

"You see that road up there on the canyon ridge?" She pointed to the road that curved up in the distance.

"Yup."

"Pretty soon a jeep or two will be coming round from Prisoners Harbor, and my friend will be on one of them, returning from a kayak excursion." She continued whispering, just in case.

"So?"

"You could flag him down, pretend to need help."

"Help? What kind of help?"

"A bandage. You could be bleeding. They'd take you to the infirmary down at the resort. You'd get to see everything, firsthand."

"Only one problem with that. I'm not bleeding."

"That's easy enough to fix." She grinned.

"You're scary."

"Or limping. Maybe you twisted your ankle and need ice." She threw up her hands. "Never mind. I'm sorry. You're right. It's a stupid idea. I'll just stick to my original plan." She turned on her heels and continued toward the resort.

He grabbed her arm. "Hang on. Suppose I do it. Then what?"

"Then you'd pass on a message to my friend."

"And how exactly am I to do that?"

"I'll write a note, asking him to meet me later tonight."

"And then what if I end up trapped there, at the resort?"

"Well, first of all, you're not a patient, so they'd have no reason to keep you there. And second of all, if they *did* keep you there against your will, well, my friend's mother is coming for me in two days with the police. She came once before, but my friend refused to go home with her."

"I see. So once I'm all done in the infirmary, assuming they let me go, I should get on with my hike? Or should I go looking for you?"

"That's up to you. Either way, I'll see you back at camp."

"And what about your friend?"

"Hopefully he'll be there with me."

"This friend of yours…is he your boyfriend?"

Daphne laughed, and, out loud, she said, "No. He's like a brother to me."

"Good."

She got the feeling Bill was hinting at something. Was he interested in Daphne? She knew she was a horrible person for thinking this, but, if he were interested, maybe he'd be more inclined to help her. And if he helped her, she might actually have a fighting chance at saving Cam.

She dropped her pack and unzipped it. Finding a piece of paper and pen, she wrote out a note to Cam: "Meet me at the Prisoners Harbor outhouse tonight. Daphne."

He narrowed his eyes.

"That's my real name. I'm sorry I lied before."

"Yeah. Why would you lie to me?"

"Because of the cameras," she whispered. "I didn't want to take a chance of being overheard." She folded the note and handed it over to him. "Cam is blond with blue eyes. He's tall and lanky like you, about your build, and not quite your age."

"You're incredibly beautiful and interesting, Daphne, and this could be the adventure I've been looking for." He stuck the paper in his trouser pocket. "But I hope I won't regret it."

She watched him hike up the hill toward the road, a bit terrified that her fate was now in his hands, but also a bit relieved. She heaved on her pack and ran toward the copse of trees to wait.

CHAPTER SIX

Abduction at Prisoners Harbor

Daphne sat on the ground behind a rock in the dark at Prisoners Harbor. Shrouded in shrubs, she was well-hidden and yet had a clear view of the outhouse and the trail leading up to it. She'd been sitting here for hours. Luckily, she'd brought along her Jetboil stove and had been able to make herself a can of beans. She'd also drank quite a lot of water—so much so that she needed to use the restroom, but every time she'd thought about using it, she'd worried that would be the very minute Cam would appear.

Unable to wait any longer, she made a dash for the outhouse. When she was finishing up, she heard someone approach. She cracked open the door to see the Australian waiting there.

"Oh, it's you," she said.

"Have you been waiting here all this time?"

"Just over there." She pointed to her rock. "Did you give him my note?"

"Yep."

"You think he's coming?"

"Dunno. Want me to wait with you?"

"Sure."

She led him to the spot that had been her camp for the past several hours. They sat side by side with their backs against the rock. Once the sun had gone down, it had become chilly on the island, and she hadn't brought her sweatshirt. A warm body beside her made a difference.

"At least there's a view from here," he said, pointing to the horizon, barely visible in the moonlight. "It hasn't been a complete waste."

She hadn't been able to enjoy the view. Her nerves had been rattled. "So what happened back at the resort? How did you give Cam my note?"

"I slipped it to him with a small tip, since he helped me into the infirmary."

"Did he open it and read it in front of you?"

"No. He left the room with it. I didn't see him again."

Surely Cam would have opened and read it. "Then what happened?"

"The doc gave me an ice pack and some pain relievers and offered to have someone drive me back here."

"So where have you been all this time?"

"Right as the driver was about to pull away from the building, another doctor came out to the jeep and gave me the third degree."

"What did the doctor look like?"

"African American woman, late thirties or early forties. A real beaut."

"Dr. Gray." Daphne bit her lip. "So what do you mean by 'the third degree'?"

"She bailed up and bloody interrogated me. Wanted to know who I was and what I was doing on the island, how long I'd been here, and if I was travelling alone."

"And what did you say?"

"Basically, the same things I told you, except for one extra detail."

"What?"

"I said my wife was with me."

Daphne blushed. The way he looked at her made it obvious he was flirting with her. Part of her wanted to tell him about Brock, to set the record straight; but another part wanted him to like her so he would help her. And boy oh boy, did she need help.

"Where did you go then?"

"The woman climbed in the backseat of the jeep, wanting to see my campsite. Quite a stickybeak, if you ask me."

"Seriously?"

"So the driver—Roger was the bloke's name, I believe—came around to our campsite. They wanted to know who else was pitched up there. I told them I didn't really know the others because they'd been off exploring the island."

"Dr. Gray and Roger didn't go inside my tent, did they?"

"Yes, the woman did. She searched every single one, except for mine. I stood in front and wouldn't let her by."

"She searched my tent?"

"I tried to stop her. I said, 'Hey, that's someone's private things,' and she just grinned at me like a shot fox and said, 'It's okay. I'm a doctor.'"

Daphne slapped her hand against her thigh. "The gall of that woman."

She tried to think of everything she'd left behind and whether any of it could have identified her as the owner.

"They left shortly after that, but I didn't want to come looking for you straight away. I had the strange feeling they were watching me. So I ate some of my dried mystery bags and…"

"Your what?"

"Sorry. Sausages. For lunch. And then I hung about like a bludger until dark."

"Do you think they're still watching you?"

"Dunno, but I see what you mean. There's definitely something shonky about that place and those people."

He didn't know the half of it, she thought.

"So what's your plan, Sweet Pea?" he asked.

Just as she started to lay out the plan for him, a jeep pulled up. Even in the dark, Cam was easy to spot behind the wheel. Thank God he had come alone—unless there were others watching from a distance. Her stomach clenched.

Full of nerves, Daphne dug out her bottle of chloroform and handkerchief and held her breath as Cam climbed from the jeep and neared the outhouse.

Cam first inspected the perimeter of the small building before opening the door to have a peek inside. As he was standing there with the door ajar, Daphne crept forward and kicked his legs out from under him. Then she straddled his waist and pressed the chloroform against his mouth. He shoved at her and punched a hard blow to her shoulder, but she held on tight with her legs. Bill swept in and pinned down Cam's arms. Daphne watched in horror as Cam strained his eyes wide open and shouted into the cloth. After a few terrifying moments, his eyes closed, and his face fell to one side.

"He's a lot bloody bigger than you made him out to be," Bill said, panting.

"I really thought you were about the same size."

"Not quite."

Now that the two guys were side by side, she could see that Bill was at least three inches shorter and not nearly as thick in the shoulders and chest, but their legs were about the same size and length.

"Now what?" he asked.

"We drag him back to my tent."

"That's a half a mile!"

"Please?"

"You'll scrape the skin off him, dragging him along the ground—not to mention bruising and grass burrs. I thought you said he was your best friend."

"He is."

"I'll have to carry him."

Daphne lifted her chin. "Can you? That would be amazing."

"At least some of the way." As Bill leaned over and grabbed Cam's torso, he said, "He's no ankle biter." Once Bill had Cam over one shoulder, he groaned and exclaimed, "He's built like a brick shit house."

"I'm sorry but keep your voice down. We don't want to draw attention."

"Yes, we do. I need help."

"You can do it, Bill. Come on."

Bill staggered under Cam's weight while Daphne carried both of their packs—which were manageable independently, but, when combined, made Daphne feel like Bill wasn't much worse off than she was.

"It's too bad we can't take the jeep," Daphne said, not sure how far she would make it before collapsing.

The trail to the campsite was too uneven and not wide enough for the vehicle.

"We better bloody try," Bill said, grunting. "Or you'll have two dead blokes."

Bill laid Cam down on the backseat. The keys weren't in the ignition. Daphne found them in Cam's jeans' pocket. She stashed the packs in the back with Cam and then she got behind the wheel.

"Let's hope this works," she said.

She eased the jeep along the trail but had to veer off when the trees left no room. The jeep jostled hard to one side, nearly toppling over, and Daphne screamed. Once she had steadied the jeep again, Bill was taken by surprise when Cam woke up and tried to strangle him. Daphne screamed again and slammed on the brakes, causing them all to fall forward and back. When Cam fell back, he broke away from Bill. Daphne fumbled for the chloroform and handkerchief, and with Bill's help, managed to get the soaked cloth over Cam's mouth again. He fell limp in the backseat.

"You got something to tie him up with?" Bill asked.

"Yes, but I don't think I should do it out in the open. What would someone think?"

"They'll think worse if we have to knock him out again."

Daphne climbed from the jeep and rummaged for her rope. Bill took it from her and tied Cam's wrists behind his back.

"Let's hope it's dark enough that no one notices," Bill said, finishing the knot before returning to the passenger's side.

Daphne got behind the wheel and started up the jeep. Navigating through the bumps and trees took them as long as it would have taken them to walk, but they managed to get the jeep within twenty feet of the tent area before they had to abandon it and carry Cam the rest of the way.

"Everything okay?" a man said, popping his head from a nearby tent.

"My cobber's just off his face," Bill said. "Too much grog, poor bloke."

Daphne let go of the breath she'd been holding when the man's head disappeared again and she and Bill managed to get Cam into her tent.

They had just got him on his side on Daphne's sleeping bag when Cam opened his eyes and said, "I'm gonna be sick."

"Not in here!" Daphne cried, glancing around for something to catch it in. If he threw up, she'd never get the smell out, and she'd be stuck with it for days.

As much as she cringed at the thought of it, she found the mug from her Jetboil stove and shoved it beside Cam's mouth. He dry heaved twice. Thank God nothing came out.

"Why are you doing this, Daphne?" Cam asked. "This isn't an exercise, is it?"

She was shocked that he would even consider that possibility. She supposed it only proved how deeply brainwashed he was. He was ready to believe anything could be for the sake of Dr. Gray's therapy.

"This isn't an exercise," Daphne said. "I'm here to rescue you."

"Aren't you a little short for a storm trooper?" Cam said. "This is some rescue."

"She's the brains, sweetheart," Bill said with a smirk.

Daphne groaned. "Look, your mom sent a professional deprogrammer out here when you wouldn't leave with her and the police."

"Deprogrammer?" Cam looked first at Daphne and then at Bill. "What the heck is a deprogrammer?"

"Come on, mate," Bill said. "Even I know… Wait. Is that like a computer whiz?"

"It's someone who helps people who've been brainwashed to get unbrainwashed," Daphne explained. "Apparently it's expensive to hire one."

"But I'm not brainwashed," Cam said. "My mom's just upset that I don't want to come home, and I don't blame her, but I've found my calling here. She has to let me spread my wings. I'm my own man and can't be controlled by her anymore."

"She's not trying to control you," Daphne said. "She's afraid for you. And so am I."

"Will you please untie me? This isn't the most comfortable position."

"Not yet. I'm sorry, but I know you'll run back to that jeep and…"

"You do realize that when they find it missing in the morning, they'll come looking for it," Cam warned.

Daphne hadn't thought of that. She looked at Bill, and he returned her worried expression.

"We're gonna have to make a run for it tonight," she said.

"Now wait a minute," Bill said. "Wouldn't it be easier if I just drove the jeep back over to the resort and hiked back?"

"Yes, except they're eventually gonna put two and two together," Daphne said. "They'll realize it was no coincidence that Cam disappeared right after you showed up. They followed you here and know where to find us. We've got to hide somewhere else, as soon as possible."

"And just where do you propose we hide?" Bill asked.

"On this side of the island, where there are other people not associated with Gomez and Gray," Daphne said. "Maybe over by Smuggler's Cove or Potato Harbor."

Bill frowned. "But I want to see the Chumash ruins. I've already been all over the national park."

"Isn't this more important?" Daphne couldn't believe what Bill was saying.

"Maybe to you, but I don't know these people. I'm beginning to regret getting involved."

"I don't blame you," Cam said. "Daphne's really lost it."

"*You're* the one who's lost it," Daphne said. "Dr. Gray has gone too far. Don't you see that, Cam? Giovanni told me Emma's death wasn't an accident. And they're going after Toni next."

"Wait, when did you talk to Giovanni?" Cam asked.

"Yesterday. He's trying to get off the island."

"Giovanni is having a hard time dealing with Emma's accident. He doesn't want to believe that bad stuff just happens. It's easier for him to blame the doctors than to believe in his own helplessness."

"Holey dooley! That's good oil."

"It's a bunch of nonsense," Daphne said. "Mumbo jumbo you've been brainwashed to believe. Giovanni overheard the three doctors. They said Emma was a *grand finale*, for the benefit of the watchers, and they wanted another, so Toni was next. It's all for money."

"Wait a minute," Bill said. He picked at his beard, like he was trying to figure something out.

"It's all a show," Daphne explained. "They have cameras everywhere so their clients—the watchers—can view the games like reality TV. It's how the doctors fund their therapy."

"And you're freakin' Katniss Everdeen," the Australian said.

Daphne's mouth dropped open. First Daphne was the Lady of Shalott, and now she was Katniss Everdeen?

No. She was Daphne Janus, with dragon flames.

"What happened to you?" Cam asked. "When you left last summer, you were happy. You recognized what Dr. Gray and her therapy did for you and for your entire family. What's changed?"

"I just realized that I'd been manipulated into choosing the rose," Daphne explained. "There's this thing called the Stockholm syndrome, where kidnapped victims…"

"You mean like me?" Cam lifted his chin and glared at her.

"Cam…"

"Face it, Daph. You're the bad guy, here. Not Dr. Gray."

"Not true!"

"You knocked me out twice and have me tied up—rather uncomfortably, I might add—against my will. And you want me to believe you're the good guy?"

"I just need to talk some sense into you."

"None of this is making any sense," Bill said.

"Bill, please." Daphne put a hand on the Australian's shoulder. "Please don't stop helping me. I'll even pay you. Cam's mom will probably want to give you a reward, too."

"I'm not motivated by money," Bill said. "My parents left me plenty."

Daphne reached over and took his hand. "Will you do it just out of the kindness of your heart, because people are in trouble and it's the right thing to do?" Then she added. "For me?"

"Where's Brock?" Cam asked. "I'm surprised he didn't come with you."

"Who's Brock?" Bill pulled his hand away from Daphne.

"My ex-boyfriend."

"Ex?" Cam tried to sit up. "God, Daph. What happened?"

"I don't want to get into it," she said, as blood rushed to her cheeks.

The mixture of concern and hope on Cam's face alarmed her, but she had already gone too far with her story to turn back now.

"Look, I need to get out of here," she said to Bill. "Are you coming with me or not?"

"It doesn't matter if he helps you," Cam said. "I'm not going anywhere."

Bill rifled through his pack and came up with a pistol. He pointed it directly at Cam. "Yes you are."

Daphne jerked back. "Oh my God! You have a gun?"

"What idiot goes backpacking in the wild without one?" Bill asked.

Daphne had considered bringing one, since all the camping websites recommended it, but had ultimately decided not to because she'd been afraid of what she might do with it. The people at the resort weren't like regular enemies; they had helped her. Their whole operation was based on the idea of helping people, even though they crossed ethical lines. Bringing a gun seemed out of the question. She'd worried she would accidentally kill someone.

"You're not going to shoot me," Cam said. "We all know it."

"Shall we find out?" Bill asked.

"No!" Daphne climbed to her knees and pushed Bill's arm toward the ground. "And be careful where you point that thing."

"Do you want my help or not?"

"Yes, but not like that. Let's just chloroform him again and carry him to the jeep."

"No!" Cam said. "Don't do that. That stuff is disgusting."

"Look, I wouldn't kill the bloke. I'd just shoot him in the foot, or…"

"And that would be smart. Then you'd have to carry him," Daphne said. "Don't shoot him at all."

"What about on his hand?"

"Are you crazy?" Cam asked. "Who is this guy, anyway, Daph? Why are you with him?"

"He's just some guy I met."

"Dear lord!" Cam cried. "Just some guy you met. That's great."

"Now hang on," the Australian complained. "The two of you are just some guys *I* met. And if you ask me who's the sanest of the group, well then…"

"Fine. Let's break down the camp and get out of here," Daphne said. "Help me drag Cam back out."

When she leaned over to grab Cam's legs, she saw something on the bottom of the tent next to the sleeping bag. She covered her mouth in shock when she realized what it was: the same type of device she'd seen on Mini-me's tail.

Daphne grabbed it and jumped from the tent. Then she dropped the device on the ground and stomped on it over and over with her boot.

Bill poked his head from the tent. "What's going on?"

"It's a camera and tracking device." She picked up the crushed object from the ground and handed it to him. "Dr. Gray must have planted it here earlier. Now she knows everything."

CHAPTER SEVEN

On the Run to Smugglers Cove

Bill tried to convince Daphne to go west, since their plans had been overheard, but Daphne was too afraid to go to the "haunted" side. The national park might be only a quarter of the island, and therefore harder to hide in, but there were other people there who could help them, and they could always catch a ride back to the mainland from Scorpion Anchorage. If they went to the west, they were more likely to run into trouble. Like the conservancy officer at the gate had said, Gomez practically owned that side of the island.

Cam refused at first to go with them, but when Daphne took out the chloroform, he climbed to his feet and followed.

They decided to abandon the jeep, because it was easier to spot and might give them away. They followed the Del Norte Trail toward the navy road for over two hours and then made their camp at the top of the hill in the woods where she and Giovanni had slept the night before.

Once the tents were set up, it was nearly midnight, and Daphne was tired and hungry. She made another pasta and chicken dish and shared it with Cam. Bill gave them a dried sausage to share, and then he returned to his tent, leaving Cam and Daphne alone.

"Please untie my hands so I can feed myself," Cam asked.

"I might in the morning, but I'm too afraid to risk it tonight."

She rinsed out her mug, offered Cam some water, and then climbed onto the sleeping bag beside him. It was cold. She wanted to climb *inside* the sleeping bag, but there wasn't enough room with the two of them. To fit, they'd have to sleep curled tightly into one another.

"So what happened with you and Brock?" he asked once she'd turned off her light. He lay on his side facing her. His hands were still tied behind his back. It was pitch dark in the tent, and she could no longer see his face.

"I told you. I don't want to talk about it." She knew the Australian could hear every word they spoke.

"Why are you doing this to me, Daphne? I thought we were friends."

"You're my best friend," she said.

"Since when do friends tie up friends?"

She laughed. "Hold on." She turned on her light. "I want to show you something."

She unzipped her pack and found the paper she was looking for. She'd stuck it in her poetry journal. She pulled it out and then lay beside him and shined the light on the paper.

"You gave this to me when you were in the fifth grade and I was in fourth."

Written on the paper was the question, "Are you my friend? Circle yes or no."

She'd been cleaning out her desk at home when she came across it. Although it had no name or date, she'd known exactly who it was from and when he'd given it to her.

"I remember that. You never gave it back to me."

Daphne took a pen from her bag and circled "yes."

"Mystery solved," she said. "I am definitely your friend."

He smiled up at her. She returned the pen and paper to her bag and clicked off her light.

"There's something you never understood about me," Cam said once she had settled beside him again in the dark.

"Your fondness for *Star Wars*?"

"Besides that. You know why I love reading and watching everything fantasy? Because this world sucks."

"This world is hard, but it doesn't suck."

"I think about the starving children in the world. The lonely people, who die alone, and no one even knows they're gone. I think of the soldiers who die at war, fighting for what?"

"Our freedom."

"But we're not free. Poverty, disease, hate, loneliness, and despair make freedom impossible. You and I, we're lucky. We grew up in wealthy households. So many other kids aren't as lucky. They starve, are malnourished, are abused, neglected, get diseases. It's too much to think about."

"Then stop thinking about it."

"I can't. Except when I'm here. When I'm on this island, helping the doctors with their work, it gives me a sense of purpose. I know I can't help every starving, diseased, lonely person suffering in this world, but I can help some, like we helped you. And we *did* help you, Daphne. You have to admit it."

"Yes." It was true. Cam had helped her. But at what price?

"And this place is exciting, too," Cam continued. "You feel alive, struggling against the elements of this island. It really makes you raw and natural and real."

"*That's* ironic. It's all a game. Nothing's real."

"It's *all* real. Every bit of it, even if it's artistic in some ways and scientific in others, it's all real. It's really happening. That's why it's called *living* art. You're both a character in a story and someone alive, living an experience."

"Just come home with me," she said. "Come home, visit your mother, and then, if you want to come back…"

His face was close to hers when he whispered, "There's only one reason I'd ever go back."

Her heart raced. She had a feeling she knew what that reason was. Before she could ask, he pressed his lips to hers.

Tears sprang to her eyes as she kissed him back. Nausea bloomed in the pit of her stomach over her betrayal to Brock, but this was the only way she could get Cam safely off the island.

"Untie me, so I can hold you," he whispered.

"Shh." She didn't want the Australian to overhear.

"Please?"

She wrapped her arms around him and held him close. His body was warm and comforting. "I don't trust you yet. Now go to sleep."

In the morning the Australian was gone. He'd left no trace behind.

"Where do you think he went?" Cam, whose hands were still tied, asked.

"He must have heard us last night. Maybe we made him feel like a third wheel."

Daphne cooked some oatmeal and spoon-fed Cam every other bite. When they'd finished it, she shared a protein bar with him.

"I'm still hungry," Cam said.

"Should I make another oatmeal packet?"

"No. I wish we had some more of that Australian's sausage. That was good."

"I have some jerky."

"Okay."

She fed him a few pieces. Then she took down the tent and packed up, while he sat watching—though he'd offered to help if she'd only untie him.

"Not yet," she'd said again.

As they headed down the trail toward Smugglers Canyon, Daphne wondered about Cam's attempt to escape with Greg—if it had been a real attempt that had failed, or if he'd been spying on Greg, as Giovanni had suspected.

"Giovanni mentioned that you tried to leave with Greg," she said, baiting him.

"That's true, but then I had a change of heart."

"This was before your mom came with the police, right?"

"Right."

"Why did you want to go in the first place? And what changed your mind?"

"Greg talked me into it."

"How?"

"He hates his mom, but he doesn't understand the importance of her work. The way he sees it, she's ruined his life and doesn't care squat about him."

A flock of seagulls screeched above them and then disappeared behind the headland.

"But that's not the way you see it?"

"Dr. Gray feels that she and Greg were both called to a higher purpose, and that comes with sacrifice."

"Don't you think Greg ought to have a choice about how he lives his life? Maybe his purpose is different from hers."

The road forked, and Daphne led them away from Scorpion Valley toward Smugglers Canyon, to the south, along Smugglers Road.

"That's exactly why I helped him. I agreed he ought to be free. And I was tired of watching Bridget use her beauty to pull the newcomers into the exercises. It was getting to me."

"But then you decided to stay."

"I realized I didn't have anything to go back home to." He met her eyes, hinting at something.

Daphne pretended not to notice. "What about your mom?"

"Last fall she wrote me a letter that she and my stepdad split up."

"So you *do* get letters here?"

"Arturo Gomez has a post office box in Ventura, and someone from the resort fetches the mail about once a month. Lately, it's been Dr. Gray, on her way back from seeing Joey."

"Oh. Well, I'd heard about your mom and stepdad. I'm sorry."

"For a long time, it was just her and me, and, man, did she lean on me—more than a mother should. That was okay, but I didn't realize how much she had absorbed my life and my energy until she met my stepdad."

"You're worried that if you go home, she'll monopolize your life?"

"Exactly. I mean, I love her, but she has to learn to live her own life. I can't be her crutch again."

"Is that why you refused to return with her when she came with the police?"

"That was one reason. I also believe in what the doctors are doing here."

They followed the road downhill and came upon the canyon ridge. According to Daphne's map, they were looking down into Smugglers Canyon, which continued toward Smugglers Cove, where there was another outhouse.

"This way," she said, leading him down into the canyon.

After a while, he said, "I still can't believe you and Brock split up."

She didn't say anything in reply.

"Do you think you'll get back together?"

"I don't know."

"Man." He laughed and shook his head. "Sorry."

"What?"

They passed beneath a clump of trees, where a few picnic tables came into view.

"It's just that, back in my junior year—when I was sixteen and you were fifteen—I had the biggest crush on you. God, you were all I ever thought about."

"I don't believe you."

"Seriously."

"You stopped coming over to play chess. You stopped inviting me to come hang out in your tree house. In fact, you talked to Kara and Joey more than you talked to me. I remember, because that was the year I finally got my braces off, and I thought, dang, he doesn't like my new teeth."

"Do you even hear yourself?" He laughed and shook his head again.

"What?"

"I got shy around you, silly. That's why I didn't hang out with you as much. I was self-conscious."

"Oh."

"Then Kara died, and well…"

"Yeah."

"And then, before I'd even blinked, you were seeing Brock. I couldn't believe it."

"I felt sorry for him. His mom had just died."

"And then I graduated, and we just stopped talking."

"But I still thought of you as my best friend."

He nodded. "I'll take that. But I thought of you as *more*."

Daphne's face filled with blood. She didn't know what to say. They reached the outhouse.

She dropped her pack. "I, um, I need to…"

"Sure."

"You promise you won't run away?"

He laughed. "Like, where would I go?"

The inside of the outhouse was covered in writing, but Daphne turned away from the declarations of love and existence and finished up quickly. When she opened the door, Cam was gone.

She scanned the beach. "Cam?"

He was sitting on the sand, a lone figure facing the sea. There were no other hikers around, just him and the lovely cove and the sunlight glimmering on the gentle waves. Daphne thought about all he'd said to her, and in her heart, she knew there was room for him. Yes, she loved Cam. She loved him as much as she loved Brock. Her grandmother had once told her that it was possible to love two men, but you had to choose one, or everyone would suffer.

She left her pack by the outhouse and padded across the beach to sit beside Cam. The sound of the gentle waves lapping against the shoreline had a calming effect, but the sharp cry of the occasional gull overhead was a reminder that things were not calm.

"It's so beautiful," she said after a few quiet moments.

"Will you please untie me now?"

"Do you promise to go home with me, and not back to the resort?"

He sighed. "Why can't you see the good of the work I do?"

"I see the good. I'm living proof of the good. I just think the price is too high."

"What price?"

She dug her heels in the sand and leaned back on her hands. "What if my dad and I would have died in that helicopter exercise?"

"But you didn't."

"We almost did."

"That's like being almost pregnant," he said.

She groaned, feeling hopeless.

After a few minutes, Cam said, "The way we see it, you and your dad were already dead. That exercise resurrected you."

She climbed to her knees and faced him. "See, that's where you're wrong. Dr. Gray's therapy wasn't our only hope."

"It was your last hope. Nothing else worked. People don't send their loved ones here unless they've tried everything else first."

"Even though my dad was depressed, maybe even suicidal, he was *alive*, and as long as he was alive, his life had *value*. Forcing him to risk his life in that helicopter exercise sent a message that his life had no value, because he wasn't living it the way you, or Dr. Gray, deemed right. Well, she's not God. She has no right to pass judgment."

"She saved his life," he said.

"Look at me."

He met her eyes. "You don't understand," he said.

"Listen to me," Daphne insisted.

"There's nothing you can say."

She kissed him, gently on the lips. Then she leaned back on her knees and asked, "Do I have your attention now?"

He smiled. "I'm listening."

"I want you to imagine something."

"Okay."

"Imagine you had just asked me to be your girlfriend."

His face turned red. "Okay."

"Now imagine that I admit that I've always loved you, too, and that I just never knew how you felt about me until it was too late."

"Is that true?"

She nodded because yes—she finally admitted to herself—it was true.

"But you and Brock are over now, right?"

"I'm not sure."

"You said you broke up."

"I'm confused, but I do know how I feel about you, and I want to know something."

"What?"

"If you and I had had our revelation before the helicopter exercise— if you'd told me you loved me, and I had told you I loved you, and if Brock had been out of the picture, be honest, would you have allowed me to get inside that helicopter?"

"I think so."

"Think hard, Cam. I could have died. Our chance for our happily ever after was at risk."

"But it was to save your father's life."

"He wasn't really dead. He was only figuratively dead. And he was already coming around because of my progress."

"Here on the island, using Dr. Gray's methods."

"Yes, but we're talking about an example of what I mean when I say she goes too far."

"All medical treatments have risks. The benefits outweighed the risks."

Daphne put her hands on his shoulders and pressed her forehead against his. She whispered, "What if Dr. Gray put me in the helicopter exercise now, to supposedly save someone else? Would you let her do it?"

"I don't know."

Daphne pressed her lips against his and gasped when he kissed her back, urgently, longingly. She felt swept up, but she pulled back.

"So you might hesitate?" she asked.

"I might hesitate."

"Because…"

"Because I'm selfish, and I wouldn't want to risk losing you. But that would be wrong."

"Why?"

"It would be wrong to put my needs before those of the greater good."

"What greater good?"

"Your father. The therapy. Dr. Gray."

"My father's needs are more important than yours?" She stood up. "Listen Cam, we're all individuals, and no one person is more important than the other. Not Dr. Gray, not my father, not me. You are just as important as anyone, and if your happiness depended on keeping me alive, then you shouldn't have to risk my life for someone else's happiness."

She crossed her arms and stared out to sea, feeling as though she was just wasting time. Cam would never see her point.

"Daphne."

She turned. He stood behind her and was mouthing something. No sound came from his mouth.

"Huh?"

He gave her an urgent look and then mouthed, "Untie me. Now."

Why wasn't he speaking?

There was only one explanation. They were being overheard. And if he was mouthing, then he was trying not to be overheard. She decided to take a chance and trust him. She worked at the rope, but it was in a tight not. She was shaking and near panic because of Cam's sense of urgency. Dang, that Australian! She needed her knife.

She ran for her backpack. Cam followed, looking utterly distraught and confused.

"Daphne!" he cried again.

She looked up from her pack and showed him her pocketknife. Then she rushed back and cut the rope binding his wrists.

He pulled a white circular device from his jean pocket and buried it in the sand. Then he strapped on her pack, took her hand, and said, "Run!"

CHAPTER EIGHT

Love and Intimidation in Scorpion Valley

Daphne glanced back to see a boat beaching in Smugglers Cove. Three people climbed out and ran toward them. Since they weren't wearing heavy backpacks, they were gaining on her and Cam.

"Faster!" Daphne cried.

Scorpion Valley, where she had set up her first camp, was at least two miles away. The uphill climb in that direction was steep, and, even without the pack, she was running out of breath. She was amazed that Cam could keep her pace while carrying her heavy load.

She glanced back toward the cove. Their three pursuers were easy to recognize now that they were within twenty feet: Vince, Dave, and Stan.

When she and Cam reached the canyon ridge, they came upon a group of hikers—a man, woman, and two little girls. The man wore a badge of some kind and carried a holster with a gun at his hip.

All she could think was *Thank God*.

"Everything all right?" the man asked.

"It is now that you're here," Cam said.

"Why were you running?" one of the little girls asked.

"Those guys back there scared us," Daphne said. "We don't know why, but they started chasing us."

The man crossed his arms. "I'm a park ranger."

"Thank God," Daphne said. "Will you help us?"

As Stan, Dave, and Vince approached, the park ranger asked them, "Do you have a permit or a campsite?"

"Are those bad guys, Daddy?" one little girl asked, as her mother picked her up and ushered her and her sister away from the scene.

"We're with the conservancy," Stan replied. "And I do have a permit." As he fumbled in his wallet he said, "How's it going, Daphne? Cam?" Then he handed a slip of paper over to the ranger.

"So you know each other?" the ranger asked.

"We're trying to get away from them," Daphne asked. "They're harassing us."

Dave scoffed, as if to suggest Daphne was lying.

"And do you have a permit or a campsite on the island?" the ranger asked Cam and Daphne.

"I'm registered to a campsite in Scorpion Valley," Daphne said. "Number thirteen."

The ranger pulled out a walkie talkie from his front pocket. "And what's your name?"

"Daphne Janus."

The park ranger spoke into the walkie talkie. "Hey, Joyce, you read me?"

"I read ya."

"Have we got a Daphne Janus registered at Scorpion Valley, number thirteen?"

"Just a minute."

Daphne took the opportunity to study Stan, Vince, and Dave, none of whom seemed to feel the least bit guilty for what they were doing. They stared back at her, but not with cruelty. It was like they felt as sorry for her as she felt for them. Stan even gave her a friendly wink. She looked away, at her boots. She'd always liked Stan. He was smart, cute, and friendly, and she really hoped she'd be able to save him.

"Yes, sir," Joyce said over the walkie talkie. "That's a ten-four."

"Thank ya, Joyce. Over and out."

"All right," the ranger said to Daphne. "You check out. Are you heading to your campsite now?"

"Yes, sir," Daphne said.

"Is that your boat?" he asked, pointing toward the cove.

"It's mine," Stan said.

"It's illegal to beach it there. We have several anchorages, and that's not one of them. I'll have to ask you to move it."

"Yes, sir," Stan said, and then, turning to Cam, said, "We'll meet up with you two later."

Daphne watched as the three boys turned and headed back down the road toward Smugglers Cove. She still felt sorry for them. Cam had been exactly like them only a few moments ago. A part of her wanted to reach out to them and tell them to come back and talk to her at her campsite.

Then she realized they probably would.

The park ranger and his family followed the three boys down the hill, and Daphne and Cam took the road in the opposite direction.

"That was close," Cam said.

"They'll be back, I'm sure." Daphne took his hand and squeezed it.

Cam held onto it. "They won't bother us as long as we're around other people."

They were above the treetops and could see the round bluff at Scorpion Anchorage from here. The sun was at high noon, and although the wind was blustery at this elevation, the sun kept them warm.

"I agree," Daphne said. "We should stay at the camp. They can't force us to go with them. And your mom should be arriving any time today or tomorrow with the police."

"My mom? She's coming here?"

Daphne nodded. "Like I said, she's worried about you."

"I'm sorry I didn't tell you about the surveillance device."

"You were only doing what you thought was right. But what finally got through to you?"

"Two things, really," he said. "Every individual has a right to happiness, even me."

"That seems so obvious. How could you forget that?"

"Dr. Gray convinced me that I was serving the greater good."

"Sacrificing yourself for a higher cause does have merit, but…"

"Now don't get me all confused."

"Her cause isn't the right one," Daphne said.

"Saving people from themselves isn't a worthy cause?"

"Not when she's willing to risk the lives of innocent people."

"Right. And that was the second thing that helped me," Cam said as the road turned east and began a sharp decline. "What you said about the lives of all people having value—even those who are so depressed that they want to die."

"How did Dr. Gray make you believe otherwise?" She kicked a rock from the trail.

"She had me convinced that a suicidal person was just going to take their life anyway, and that living with depression wasn't really living. There's some truth to that, don't you think?"

"Maybe. But it's not Dr. Gray's place to decide whose lives are worth risking—who deserves to live and who doesn't."

"Right. I need to remember that. But were we really risking their lives in a controlled exercise? Oh, Daph. I hope I didn't just screw everything up. I love this place. What have I done?"

"What about Emma? Do you believe what Giovanni said about the grand finale?"

"I don't know." He looked away, like he was thinking.

The path curved in the opposite direction for a half mile before turning east again. Then Scorpion Valley and the campsites came into view.

Daphne was relieved when they reached site number thirteen and pitched their tent among the other campers.

Tired of pasta and chicken, Daphne heated up a can of beans, and she and Cam ate the rest of the jerky with it. She expected Cam's mom to arrive either today or tomorrow—whenever the next boat came from Ventura—so there was no reason to ration out the food. They also had a source of drinking water, so she didn't hold back, like she had been doing all day, and it felt good to drink until her thirst was fully quenched.

As the sun went down, the chill factor increased, and Daphne was regretting her decision not to bring a jacket. It rarely got cold in San Antonio over spring break, and as hot as it had been on the island last summer, she hadn't been able to imagine the temperature dropping so low that she'd be uncomfortable in a sweatshirt and jeans.

But even with them on, as nighttime approached, and she and Cam waited nervously for the arrival of someone from the resort, she found her clothes weren't doing the job of keeping her warm.

"I wonder why they haven't come yet," she kept saying.

She cooked them one more meal at night—two batches of pasta chicken—and, after they ate, they made the hike together up to the out-house.

When they returned, Cam borrowed some kindling, firewood, and matches from a nearby camper and built them a fire.

"Oh, that's better," Daphne said, finally feeling her fingers again.

"I doubt they're coming tonight," Cam said.

"Maybe they hope to smuggle us out while everyone else is asleep."

"I've heard you scream, Daph. You can wake the dead."

She laughed. "That's true. So you really think we're safe?"

"It's too dangerous at night—by boat or jeep. And this wind just makes it worse. I think they'll come tomorrow."

She couldn't resist curling up against the warmth of his body. He wrapped his arms around her, and they gazed into the flames, perfectly silent and comfortable.

Before too long, Daphne found herself nodding off.

After a while, Cam said, "There's not enough wood to keep the fire going any longer."

She must have been completely out. "Huh?"

"Why don't we climb into your sleeping bag and try to get some shut-eye?"

"Sounds good."

They left the coals of their dying fire and, shivering, squeezed up against each other in the single bag. Daphne zipped them in, her teeth chattering. Then she buried her face in Cam's neck.

"I would have frozen to death without you," she said, soaking up his heat.

He kissed her forehead. "Glad to be of service."

She giggled. "That sounded bad."

He laughed. "Yes, it did."

She couldn't see his face in the darkness, but she could feel him wanting her. She shivered with the realization that if Kara had never died, she'd probably be with Cam instead of Brock.

"Daphne?" Cam whispered.

"Hmm?"

"Are you warm enough?"

"Yes. You?"

"Uh-huh."

They were quiet again, and she'd nearly fallen asleep when Cam stirred and whispered, "Daphne?"

"Hmm?"

"I love you."

She swallowed hard. "I love you, too."

Tuesday morning, Daphne opened her eyes. The sunlight both warmed and illuminated the tent. The cold from last night was beginning to dissipate. In fact, her feet were sweating in her socks, and she thought about unzipping the bag and letting out a little of their heat, but she didn't want to wake up Cam. He looked so blissful sleeping soundly beside her, his face near hers. She fought the urge to kiss him.

The sounds of footsteps along the path alarmed her when they stopped just outside her tent.

"Cameron, I know you're in there," Dr. Gray's voice came, stark in the otherwise quiet morning. "Daphne? Both of you, come on out. We need to talk."

Cam yawned, and stretched, as though he hadn't heard.

"Cam, wake up," Daphne whispered.

"Yes, Cam, do," Dr. Reynolds said.

"We don't have all day," Dr. Gray added.

"Huh?" Cam sat up, squinting.

Daphne sat up, too. "They're here."

Cam kissed the top of her head. "It's going to be okay. Okay?"

Tears sprang to her eyes. She was afraid, but she wanted to be strong. She didn't want the doctors to know how frightened she was. "Okay."

They crawled from the tent—first Cam and then Daphne—to find the others sitting at the picnic table, waiting.

"Cameron, come sit next to Stan, across from Dr. Reynolds and me," Dr. Gray said in her commanding voice. "We'd like to talk to you first."

Daphne clutched Cam's arm as he started to obey. She wanted him to remain at her side. He glanced at her, read her mind, and stayed.

They were both in their socks—their boots still lying just inside the tent. It was chilly but not cold. The sun was still far in the east, meaning it must be early. Daphne glanced at her watch. It was eight o'clock.

Stan winked at Daphne, and she gave him a sad, half smile, that said I wish things were different. She wanted him to know she was there to save him.

"Please, Cameron," Dr. Reynolds said. "Have a seat."

"I'm fine standing," Cam said.

"All right, then," Dr. Gray said. "We want you to know that we understand why you abandoned your mission."

Cam moved a few pebbles around with his toe, getting the sock dirty.

"But you might be interested to know that Daphne lied to you," Dr. Gray said.

Cam stiffened beside Daphne and his ears turned red. He searched her eyes.

"Wait a minute," Daphne said. "Lied about what?"

Dr. Reynolds replied, "We all know that you did not, in fact, end your relationship with Brock."

Cam's mouth dropped open and he took several steps back, away from Daphne. "Wait. What?"

"Cam, listen. I'm trying to help you."

"Really?" He gave her a hard, angry look. "This doesn't feel like help. Is it true?"

Daphne turned to the doctors. "How can you possibly know these personal details about my life?"

"I can't believe it," Cam said. "You lied to me."

"I sent Arturo to verify," Hortense explained. "He contacted Brock, who was not only shocked to hear you had returned to the island but was equally shocked that you would say you had broken up."

"You called Brock?" Daphne was astounded and raging mad. She glanced at Cam to see him white as a sheet, clenching fists and jaw.

"And we notified your parents, too," Dr. Gray added.

"What?" Daphne's heart raced in her chest.

Dr. Gray continued, "As you might have suspected, Cameron's mother arrived yesterday evening with a Ventura police officer."

"And they brought along someone else," Dr. Reynolds said.

Daphne felt the blood rush from her face.

Hortense Gray gave her a smug grin. "It's someone who's been quite interested in the surveillance we were able to capture of you with that man named Bill embracing in the stream, half-naked."

"The Australian?" Cam gawked.

"Not to mention the recording of you telling Cameron your true feelings for him," Lee Reynolds added.

They didn't need to say his name. Daphne knew who it was, and her heart dropped into her belly like a heavy anchor.

CHAPTER NINE

Mission Impossible

On the boat ride over from Scorpion Anchorage, Cam wouldn't even look at Daphne, who stood at the railing between Dr. Gray and Stan. Stan had offered to carry her pack, and she had let him, and Cam stood on the other side of him away from her. Daphne believed Stan wanted to prevent her from trying to explain to Cam why she had lied about Brock, which is exactly what she was anxious to do, as soon as possible. If only she could make him understand that she'd needed the Australian's help, and that she had never intended to lie to Cam, maybe he wouldn't be as hurt. She worried Cam would once again refuse to return home with his mother, and Daphne's mission would have been for nothing.

The whole time she had packed up her tent back at the campsite, Cam had refused to look at her, and every time she had tried to speak to him, one of the doctors had interrupted her with a barrage of questions, such as, "Did you think to bring a first aid kit in case you were injured?" and "What do you think your parents will say? We were obligated to contact them, you know." Worst of all had been, "This could be a major setback for your brother, who still fears you blame him for Kara's death."

Daphne had wanted to scream.

When Dr. Gray was busy talking with Dr. Reynolds, Daphne tried once more to get around Stan and her bulky pack.

"Listen to me, Cam."

He ignored her.

"The Australian wouldn't help me otherwise. I never meant to hurt you."

Cam either couldn't hear her over the boat engine and the thrash of the waves, or he was pretending he couldn't.

"Better hold on to the railing, Daphne," Dr. Gray called out to her. "We wouldn't want you to get hurt."

Seething with anger, she ignored Hortense Gray and shouted, "Cam! Look at me!"

It was Stan who turned around to face Daphne. "Come on, kiddo. Give him some time."

Daphne fought the tears building in her eyes and returned to the railing, but she refused to hold on to it. She had to spite Dr. Gray every little way possible. If she could, she would punch the woman in the face, because she had no right, absolutely no right to manipulate people like this.

Daphne was about to say that very thing out loud, when Hortense leaned in close, with a smug look on her face and said, "I'm Prospero, remember? *I* control what goes on here. Please don't try to undermine my good work."

Daphne glared at her. "You're not God."

Dr. Gray leaned even closer, inches from Daphne's face, and said, in a low voice so no one else would overhear, "I may not be God, but I'm close. I'm more like an author. And you, my dear, are a character to be manipulated for the pleasure and healing of others, including your own."

"I write my own story," Daphne said with narrowed eyes.

Dr. Gray smiled. "Very good."

Lee Reynolds turned to Hortense and said, "The dolphins are back."

Hortense put an arm around Lee and leaned over the railing to watch the dolphins with him, laughing cheerfully, as though she hadn't just exchanged harsh words with Daphne.

Daphne wanted to scream again. Just as she was about to make one more effort to get around Stan, the boat docked at Prisoners Harbor and it was time to go ashore. Waiting for her on the end of the pier was Brock. Had he been waiting for her all morning?

When Cam noticed Brock, he turned white again and glanced toward Daphne for the first time since they'd boarded. She mouthed, "Let me explain," but he turned away from her and climbed ashore, walking stiffly past Brock without even acknowledging him.

That's when Daphne noticed Mrs. Turner at the top of the bluff. When Cam reached the top of the steps, he was embraced by his mother before they both climbed into the jeep with a police officer and Roger. If they spoke, Daphne couldn't hear them over the squawking of the pelicans.

She followed Stan onto the pier and approached Brock warily, trying to read his expression.

He fell in line beside her as they followed Stan up the steps to the top of the bluff.

"Before you say anything, will you hear me out?" she asked.

She couldn't whisper and be heard over the pelicans, but she tried to speak as softly as possible, so as not to be interrupted by the doctors behind her.

"I don't know what makes me angrier," Brock said. "The fact that you returned to this place, or the fact that you didn't trust me enough to tell me about it."

"Are you going to listen to me or not?" she asked.

"So *now* you want to talk. You couldn't talk to me *before* you came back here?"

She said nothing more as they followed Stan up to a second jeep, which the rest of them piled into. Daphne sat wedged between Dr. Gray and Brock. She balled her fists.

"You've got no right to treat people like this," Daphne finally said to Dr. Gray as they reached the canyon ridge on their way to the resort.

"I'm not the one who lied to three men in three days," Dr. Gray replied.

Brock crossed his arms but said nothing. Daphne felt like she was on the verge of losing all control.

"Oh, you've lied to many more men than that," Daphne accused.

"If you mean my practice of using the element of surprise with the patients I treat here, well, we've already discussed the importance of that," Dr. Gray said. "But, unlike you, I don't lie to my friends."

Daphne gritted her teeth. "That's because you don't have any."

"I'm her friend," Lee Reynolds said from the passenger seat.

"I am, too," Stan said from behind the wheel.

Dr. Gray smiled and asked, "And, outside of your therapy, have I ever once lied to either of you?"

"Nope," Stan said.

"Not once," Lee added.

"And have I ever tried to use my sexuality to get you to do something you didn't want to do?" Hortense asked.

"Nope," Stan said as they reached the resort and he pulled into the clearing to park.

"I wish," Lee replied with a snort.

"So perhaps Miss Janus isn't as well on the road to recovery as we once believed," Dr. Gray said with a facetious tone, her hand on the door. "Maybe she needs more therapy, to learn how to treat her friends properly."

Daphne was appalled that Brock hadn't said a word to defend her, but before she could make a reply in her own defense, everyone climbed from the vehicle.

Quickly, she scooted over the seat to exit on Brock's side. She ran up to him, took one of his hands, and said, "Please let me explain."

He gave her a sad smile and cupped her cheek with one hand. "You can tell me about it on the boat ride home, okay?"

Filled with relief she embraced him. "But we can't leave without Cam, okay?"

"What do you mean we can't leave without Cam?" He searched her face.

"He's the whole reason I came here."

"But if he chooses to stay, that's his choice. I've got to get back to school next week. I can't take an extended vacation. I've got a swim meet on Saturday. I was supposed to be at practice today as it is."

They caught up with the others, who had begun descending the path down into the resort.

Roger was saying, "The next boat back to the mainland meets at Prisoners Harbor at four this afternoon, officer."

"That works for me," the officer said.

"We can feed you lunch before you go," Hortense added. "You, too, Pamela, unless you plan to stay."

Mrs. Turner's eyes were red-rimmed. "Can I have some private time with my son?"

"Take as much time as you need," Hortense replied. "If you decide to stay, you'll need to check in with the front desk in the lobby of the main building and make your payment by check or credit card. Brock and Daphne, that goes for you, too."

Brock pulled Daphne aside. "I can't afford to stay another night. They charged me $450 last night, for me alone."

"Mrs. Turner didn't pay for you?" Daphne asked.

"She offered, but it didn't seem right."

Stan dropped Daphne's pack at her feet. "It was good to see you again, kiddo."

Then he turned and followed the doctors to the main building, leaving Cam and his mom, and Daphne and Brock behind on the sidewalk outside the cabanas.

"How can this be?" Mrs. Turner said to Cam. She turned her eyes on Daphne. "You couldn't talk any sense into him either?"

"I'm sorry," Daphne said. "For a little while, we had him. I reminded him that his needs are as important as anyone's."

"That's right, sweet boy," Cam's mom said as the tears broke.

"And Dr. Gray doesn't have the right to decide whose lives have value and whose is worth risking, even if she considers someone *figuratively* dead," Daphne continued.

"Figuratively dead?" Mrs. Turner asked. But Daphne went on without explaining what she meant.

"She's not God, and although sacrificing for the greater good for some causes is a good thing, this is not a good cause, because Dr. Gray goes too far. Remember, Cam? You agreed with me. Remember? Think of Emma."

He finally looked at her, with narrowed his eyes. "And why should I trust someone who lied to me and broke my heart?"

"Oh, dear," Mrs. Turner said, covering her mouth.

"I never meant to lie to you," Daphne said.

"All that talk about loving me," Cam added.

"But I do love you. That part was true." She glanced back at Brock and then moved closer to Cam. "I did love you all those years. And I do love you now. But the only reason I said that Brock was my *ex-*boyfriend was to get the Australian to help me, so I could help you."

Cam's bottom lip trembled, and he stepped so close that she could feel the denim of his jeans on the back of her hand. He looked down at her with fire and hate and spoke through gritted teeth. "What you did to me was worse than anything these doctors have ever done. Why should I go back with you? This place helps me forget."

He turned on his heels and walked away.

"Cameron, wait!" Mrs. Turner rushed to catch up with her angry son.

Daphne turned back to Brock.

When she didn't say anything, he laughed and asked, "So you have nothing to say to me after that?"

"What can I say?" Tears spilled from her eyes. She was tired and emotionally spent, and she almost didn't give a damn about anything at this point. Her mission had failed, and she'd only made everything worse instead of better. "What I said to Cam is true. I loved him when we were kids, and I love him now. But I love you, too. And you're the one I want to be with."

"How do I know you won't change your mind later and decide you'd rather be with him?"

She let out the breath she'd been holding, and a nervous laugh escaped with it. "Aside from my word, which I know means nothing anymore, you won't."

He moved over to her and cupped her face in his hands. "Daphne, come home with me now. Come away from this island and go home where it's safe."

She looked up at him, speechless. What could she say?

Brock wiped her tears with his thumbs. "Cam is a grown man. And his mother is here. There's nothing more you can do for him. If you stay, you know what will happen. You'll get pulled into another B.S. exercise that might just kill you."

Tears poured from her eyes. She felt responsible for Cam in the same way she felt responsible for Joey. She wasn't sure why. Maybe because his happiness had depended on her, and she'd let him down. Maybe because she loved him. Yes, that was it. She wanted to spend her life with Brock, but she did love Cam, and she couldn't just leave him here to be used and manipulated.

She became conscious of a surveillance camera on the upper corner of a nearby cabana. It was trained directly on her. She looked up at it with hate at the watchers on the other end. She couldn't see them, and she didn't even know who they were, but knowing they were getting pleasure out of her struggle filled her with rage.

"Come back with me to my room and wash up," Brock said. "Maybe it will help clear your mind. Then we'll eat some lunch. You'll feel better then."

CHAPTER TEN

Malcolm Gray's Journal

The warm shower did make a difference, Daphne thought, as she slipped on her last clean clothes—a pair of shorts and a t-shirt. Brock gave her a fresh pair of his socks to wear with her boots. Although she'd been rinsing her mouth with mouthwash, it felt good to actually brush her teeth. And pulling her comb through clean, silky hair seemed like a long-lost luxury after two days of wearing a stringy mop.

When she came from the bathroom, Brock, who was sitting on one of two chairs in the sitting area, looked up at her and smiled.

"Feel better?"

"Uh-huh," she said.

"You look better, too."

She took the chair beside him. "You haven't said anything yet about my hair."

"You look great in any color."

"But you prefer me as a brunette." She could tell. He didn't have to say it.

"I'm just not used to it, that's all." He took her hand. "I think you're beautiful even without hair, remember?"

She frowned—not because of what he said, but because of the memory it brought on. Her Limuw ceremony had been emotional, and she supposed she still hadn't come to terms with how she felt about the supposed therapy she had received here. Yes, it showed her how much she had to live for. Yes, it helped her brother come out of his psychosis into a more normal range for mental health, but she couldn't think about it without feeling victimized, too.

Brock squeezed her hand and pulled her onto his lap. "You have no idea how terrifying that was for me," he said. "To get a call from Arturo Gomez claiming you'd returned to the island."

"I'm so sorry." She kissed the top of his head. "What did you say?"

"What you told me. That you were on spring break with a friend. Then I called that place in Galveston and they'd never hear of you or Mandy."

"Did you tell my parents?"

"I had to."

"That's exactly why I didn't tell you in the first place. Plus, I knew you'd try to talk me out of coming."

"Of course. This was crazy, Daph. You see that now, right?"

Her stomach clenched. "Mrs. Turner needed help, and she had no one else."

"You were in no position to help. You're a seventeen-year-old girl. What did you expect to accomplish here?"

"I, I…" She was going to say she was almost eighteen but couldn't get it out.

"This is a powerful operation, run by wealthy investors and clever doctors," Brock continued. "Did you really think you could outsmart them all?"

Daphne climbed from his lap, at a loss. "What are you saying? Are you saying you don't have faith in me?"

She had dragon flames!

He stood up. "No, of course that's not what I'm saying. But if Mrs. Turner's deprogrammer couldn't do it…"

"Then you're saying I'm stupid."

"No. That's not what I'm saying."

"I bet Dr. Gray paid that de-programmer guy money to leave. He didn't care about Cam like I do. That was the difference. And I'm not stupid."

"Of course, you're not. But you were thinking with your heart, and not with your brain."

"Sometimes we have to listen to our hearts." Her stomach felt sick.

He sighed and closed his eyes for a moment. "Let's go grab some lunch."

"I'm not hungry anymore."

"Come anyway, in case you change your mind. I need to eat, and I don't want to leave you alone for one minute while we're here."

As they were about to leave, something was slipped under their door. Brock opened the door, and they saw Greg running away. The item he had left behind was a notebook.

Daphne picked up it up and turned it over. On a piece of paper taped to the notebook was written:

Take this to the restroom to avoid the cameras.

Daphne motioned to Brock. "Wanna take another shower?"

"Huh?" He followed her.

Daphne locked the bathroom door, turned on the shower, and opened the notebook. A photograph and a folded piece of paper were tucked inside.

The photo was old and slightly creased, and it showed eight children—three girls and five boys—lined up in front of a building. Inside the folded piece of paper, it read:

I'll end up paying for sharing this with you, but I wanted to explain why I'm back. My mother tracked me down over a month ago and revealed something to me that rocked my world. My father cannot know. The watchers cannot know. You must not tell a soul. Flush this paper as soon as you've read it.

Emma is alive.

Daphne and Brock gawked at one another for a minute. Daphne felt the room spin, and the floor dropped from beneath her.

"That can't be true." Daphne leaned against the bathroom vanity, her knees too weak to hold her.

"What else does it say?"

They kept reading.

The subscribers needed what they call a "grand finale," so my mom and the other doctors concocted the staged death with Emma's help. I had no idea. I left this place because I thought they had caused Emma's death. Sometime after I spoke with you, my mom tracked me down and told me the truth about Emma.

This journal belonged to my grandfather—my mother's father. I thought you might find it interesting. It explains how it's possible for me to both love and hate my mom.

Greg

"This has to be another exercise," Brock said. "We saw her with our own eyes."

"But what if he's telling the truth?" Daphne hoped he was, and it would be cruel, so cruel, for him to make them think Emma was alive only to have them mourn her loss all over again with the truth.

"Let's take a look at the journal."

She flushed Greg's note down the toilet, and then, with their backs to the mirror, they leaned against the vanity and inspected the book. Daphne turned to the first page:

May 10, 1977

Subject No. 7

Of the eight children I procured today from Madam Wesslock's Home for Orphans, this subject, a scrawny, ten-year-old black girl, is the most promising. In our initial interview, alone in Madam Wesslock's office, the subject asked if I was to be her new "Pappy."

According to her records, her parents had abandoned her five years prior to my arrival because they were too poor to give their child proper care.

I told the subject that indeed I was to be her new "Pappy."

Without further introduction, she threw her arms around my neck and declared that she "loved" me.

Daphne met Brock's eyes. "How sad."

"Yeah."

"Keep reading?"

Brock nodded, so Daphne turned the page.

May 14, 1977

Subject No. 7

Still reeling from the tantrum I endured from Subject No. Six, I was pleased to find this subject more cooperative. I began in the same way as I had with the others. Her room is the smallest and so lacked a proper table and chairs, but she sat on her bed and I on a folding metal chair I brought in from the garage.

I asked her to tell me everything she could recall about her past.

She said her name was Hortense Walker, and when she was four, she took care of her two-year-old brother while her "other pappy" and "momma" were at work. She did not know what her father's occupation was, but she said her mother cleaned houses, and sometimes she and her little brother went with her and either waited in the car or sat and watched television until her mother finished. But then a new baby came, and her mother stopped working. She said that when her "other pappy" got too sick to work, her "poor momma cried and cried."

Hortense was told her brother would have to go live somewhere else, because he ate too much and wasn't as helpful. At this point, the subject struggled to control her emotions, but she did not cry. Once she recovered, she reported that a few days before her fifth birthday, her mother took her to Madam Wesslock's Home for Orphans to see her brother, but he had already been adopted by another family. Here the subject once again struggled with her emotions before reporting that she was even more devastated to learn that she had been brought to the orphanage to stay. Her mother told her she couldn't take care of her anymore but promised to visit. The subject said she never had the chance to say goodbye to her "other pappy."

When I asked how often her mother had visited, the subject replied that she had only come one other time, on her sixth birthday. The mother came with the subject's baby sister. Hortense never saw them again after that visit.

I asked her to tell me about the five years she spent at Madam Wesslock's Home for Orphans. She said she made her bed every day, did her other chores, and liked to be helpful. At this point she asked if there was any way she could be helpful to me.

I told her indeed there was. I explained that I was a doctor and I wanted to practice a new kind of therapy with her, to help her overcome her difficult past. I warned her that it would involve pain. Unlike the other subjects, who were resistant to this news, she smiled and said, "Okay, Pappy."

Brock took the journal from Daphne and thumbed through the pages. "This covers the next several years of her life."

"I'm dying to finish it. Why don't you go to lunch without me?"

"I'm afraid to leave your side."

She was afraid, too, but would rather stay alone than stop reading.

Brock pushed her hair away from her eyes. "They're trying to lure you into another exercise. I just know it."

"Then stay and read with me?"

"You keep reading while I go see if there's anything to eat in the kitchen."

She gave him a quick kiss on the lips and sat down on the floor to find where she had left off in the journal.

May 20, 1977

Subject No. 7

The subject's responses to my questions were short and to the point. When asked if she felt guilty about anything in her past, she said she only wished she could have been more helpful. It seems, as in many cases like hers, she felt responsible for her parents' inability to keep her. Although financial crisis was the root cause, she be-

lieved her character to be at fault. Why victims continually blame themselves for their victimization is something that requires further exploration.

As with the other subjects, I asked her to lie prone across the bed and explained I was going to strike her three times with a belt. I was surprised when she fully cooperated. I did not have to use restraints of any kind. She lay there, as I applied my treatment to her bare back. She made no effort to avoid the sting of the belt. Although she flinched and even wept, she neither screamed nor pleaded with me to stop. I am quite pleased with her.

Daphne gasped and turned the page. The next several pages reported more of the same, but Malcolm also commented that he had "lost another subject." She wondered what that meant. Had the children run away? Committed suicide? Or had Malcolm given them back to the orphanage? Maybe he killed them. She scanned the pages but found no explanation.

Then she found an entry, dated August 8, 1980, in which Malcolm wrote that he had decided to make Hortense his protégé.

At only thirteen years of age, she has a keen grasp for the importance of psychological exploration and discovery to the future of humankind. I'm enrolling her into a private school to better her education.

Other entries stated that she was "excelling in all of her subjects" and "proved to be as intelligent as he had believed." He made her an assistant and soon allowed her to administer treatment to the other subjects. He wrote that she made an "excellent and skilled assistant." Before graduating from high school, she was accepted into Princeton University's School of Psychology, which he wrote "pleased him immensely."

Brock returned to the bathroom with a plate of sandwiches and two cans of coke. While they ate, she told him what she had discovered in the journal.

"Well, that explains a lot," he said.

Daphne continued to skim through the pages as they ate.

"Here Malcolm writes that she's 'developed a fixation on the works of Nietzsche,'" Daphne said. "He says, 'Hortense's new fascination with the interplay between science and art will distract her, I'm afraid, from pure clinical trials. She may prove to be a disappointment to me yet.'"

"How cruel," Brock said. "It's like he had no heart."

"I know. I wonder how it must have felt for her to read this."

"I can't imagine," Brock said as he finished up the last of his sandwiches.

"Oh, wow!" Daphne said. "Listen to this! She took over in the journal."

May 20, 1989

Hortense Gray

I have just graduated from Princeton, summa cum laude, *with a degree in psychology. My father did not live long enough to see me walk the stage, but at least I was able to tell him before he died that I was accepted into graduate school at Harvard.*

"She doesn't say how he died?" Brock asked.

Daphne skimmed down the page. "Uh-uh. I don't think so."

"Maybe she killed him." he said.

"No way."

"I'm just kidding. But I wouldn't have blamed her. What a jerk."

"She says here, 'My father was a great man. I plan to continue his legacy without compromising my own interest in what I am calling living art. Freud once wrote that the child, reluctant to give up a source of pleasure, wants to continue childhood play but feels ashamed to do so as an adult. Art becomes the socially acceptable way for an adult to continue play.'"

"Does she talk about how she started this place?" Brock asked.

"I haven't come across that yet, but there are still more pages. Let me see."

A loud knock at the front door made her flinch.

"Should I answer it?" Brock asked.

"I don't know."

He stood up, but before he could open the bathroom door, they heard the outside door swing open against the wall. Brock reached over and locked the bathroom door as Daphne climbed to her feet.

"Daphne? Brock?" It was Stan. "Dr. Gray sent me to check on you. What are you two doing in the bathroom?"

Brock glanced back at Daphne, who shrugged. She stuffed the journal into one of the vanity drawers. Then she turned off the shower.

Brock said, "What do you think two teens who haven't seen each other in three days would be doing together in the bathroom? Can you come back later?"

Daphne wet her hand beneath the faucet and ran moisture through her hair, shaking it into a mess. "I'm almost dressed!"

"You need to either check out or pay for another night," Stan said. "The boat leaves from Prisoners Harbor in less than an hour."

"We're checking out. Thanks," Brock called out as he, too, ran some water through his hair.

"Then can I help you with your bags?" Stan called through the door.

Daphne opened it. "Hey, Stan."

"Hey. Sorry to interrupt."

Blood rushed to her face. "That's okay. Listen, I wanted to say goodbye to you before we go, so I'm glad you came by."

"That's good news. I had the feeling you didn't like me anymore."

She frowned. "Of course, I like you. I just don't agree with what you do here."

"I'm sorry to hear that."

"The concept is good, but you guys go too far. You risk the lives of innocent people. I don't think that's right."

"There's a lot you don't understand about this place, kiddo." He patted her shoulder. "Take care of yourself."

"You, too."

He turned to leave, but before he stepped from the unit she said, "Stan?"

"Yeah?"

"Have you ever thought about leaving this place and living a normal life?"

"We help a lot of people here, Daphne. I can't imagine a more satisfying life than that."

He left before she could reply.

<u>CHAPTER ELEVEN</u>

Mary Ellen Rose

Daphne was surprised by the appearance of Mary Ellen Rose just as Stan left Brock's unit. The doctor stood on the porch, frowning.

"What a surprise," Daphne said, feeling uneasy.

"I know you weren't expecting me, hon, but I was wondering if you would walk with me to the main building. I'd like a word with you."

Brock put a protective arm around Daphne.

"You're welcome to come, too, dear," Mary Ellen said to Brock.

Seeing no reason not to follow her, Brock and Daphne closed the door behind them and stepped out into the sunny afternoon. She was worried about Malcolm Gray's journal, which was still in the bathroom drawer. If someone watching the surveillance wanted to see what Greg had slid under her door, would they go back and search Brock's unit while she and Brock were with Dr. Rose? Daphne began to believe that Mary Ellen's motive for taking them to the main building was to lure them away from Brock's room so others could investigate. What if she just got Greg into serious trouble?

They walked side by side, with Daphne in the middle. The wind was gentle, and the sun was bright. It shone directly above them in a clear blue sky with a handful of gulls for company.

As Mary Ellen waddled along the sidewalk, she said, "I was troubled by some of the things you said to Cameron before he destroyed the surveillance device, and I hoped for an opportunity to talk to you."

"Okay," Daphne said as they crossed the sidewalk toward the entrance to the main building.

"You spoke to Cam about his being brainwashed, but I want you to understand something. Indoctrination and enlightenment look a lot alike."

"What do you mean?" Brock asked.

"I mean, it's not always easy to tell when one is being indoctrinated into a bogus system of belief or being shown the truth," Mary Ellen said. "Just think about that for a bit."

Daphne wasn't sure what to say.

"And for another thing, nearly all forms of medical treatment come with risks," she said. "When a patient asks to be put on antidepressants, for example, there's a chance the medication will eventually destroy his liver."

"I get that," Daphne said.

"There's even a small percentage of the population that might have a fatal reaction to the medication," Mary Ellen continued. "But if the symptoms are bad enough, the doctor will take the chance and prescribe the medication anyway. Do you understand what I'm saying, hon?"

As they neared the doors to the building, Brock opened them, and they all three entered the foyer. Mrs. Turner was standing with Cam by the leather loungers, full of tears. They were arguing. Daphne avoided their eyes and turned back to Mary Ellen.

"Yes, I do understand," Daphne said.

Dr. Rose led them to the elevators and pushed the "up" arrow. "And so when you say that our program goes too far because it risks people's lives, well, I'd like you to rethink that, given that *most* treatment entails risk."

The elevator doors opened. Daphne breathed in and out, searching for her happy place. She could do this, she reminded herself as she stepped inside. She had dragon flames!

Brock squeezed her hand and followed her inside.

"You okay?" he whispered.

Daphne nodded.

"And, for another thing, when you said that Cameron's needs were as important as anyone else's," Mary Ellen said as the elevator doors closed, "we couldn't agree more. But what you don't acknowledge is the benefit for Cameron as he works toward a higher purpose. This feeling of purpose fills him with joy, even if at times he risks losing people he loves."

The elevator doors opened on the second floor, and Daphne let out the breath she'd been holding as they stepped out.

"Not unlike soldiers who carry out missions in battle," Mary Ellen added.

Brock held the elevator doors for the ladies as they stepped out. "But this isn't war."

"It most certainly is," Mary Ellen objected, gesturing for them to continue down the hallway. "It's absolutely war. A war on mental illness and depression. A war against suicide. Do you know how many people take their lives each year?"

Daphne glanced at Brock. They both shook their heads.

"Over forty-thousand people in America alone," Mary Ellen said, as she inserted the key into the door of her office. "We don't have enough data to know how bad it is globally, but that's already a lot of people. Wouldn't you agree?"

They both nodded.

She opened the door and ushered them in. "In fact, twice as many people die each year from suicide as they do from AIDS."

"I didn't know that either," Daphne said.

Mary Ellen's office was much better organized than Hortense Gray's. There were no extraneous paintings, looms, books, and records placed in every little nook or cranny. There were paintings, but they were tastefully hung. There were also books, but each had a space on the wall of shelves around the window.

"And for young people, aged 15-24," the doctor continued, "suicide is the second leading cause of death. Did you know that?"

Both teens shook their heads.

"One person dies by suicide every fourteen minutes," the doctor added, lifting both palms in the air. "So, yes. This most certainly is a war."

"I apologize," Brock said. "I stand corrected."

"Here's one more statistic for you," Mary Ellen said. "Twenty percent of people who seek help for depression still follow through with suicide. But here, at our facility, we save one hundred percent of our patients."

"What about Emma?" Daphne asked, still not sure if she should believe Greg's note.

"Please follow me." Mary Ellen opened the door leading to the surveillance room.

Lee Reynolds looked up from his desk and removed his headset. "Oh, hello. What do we have here?"

Mary Ellen closed the door leading to her office. "I'm sure you've overheard the information I've just given these two young people, Lee. Would you agree that those statistics are accurate?"

"Yes," Lee Reynolds replied, "according to the Center for Disease Control."

Mary Ellen went to a control board and turned several switches.

"What are you doing?" Lee asked her.

"I want to explain something to them without being overheard," Mary Ellen said.

Lee stood up. "Are you sure…"

"I'm positive," Mary Ellen interrupted as she turned to face the teens. "In spite of my hard work and dedication to this facility, I want you two to know that I do not approve of the new direction our practice has taken. The needs of the investors have come to mean more to our operation than the needs of the patients, which is why Emma's life was put into terrible jeopardy."

"Don't do this." Lee lurched forward and cupped a hand over Mary Ellen's mouth.

Brock intervened by twisting one of Lee's arms behind his back.

"Let the woman finish," Brock insisted.

Lee struggled against Brock for a moment, but the thin doctor was no match for Brock.

"Come on, Lee." Mary Ellen was shaking and panting. "You agree with me. I know you do. You're just too afraid to stand up to her."

"She doesn't like it any more than we do," Lee said. "But she's right when she says we can't make it without funding. The expenses have gotten out of hand."

"Then we cut them," Mary Ellen said. "We don't need a helicopter and a private boat. And we can open the resort up to regular tourists, like we did in the beginning. There are many ways we could save money."

Daphne wasn't sure what to say. She and Brock exchanged looks of confusion.

"I'd hate to see this place shut down." Tears welled in Mary Ellen's eyes. "After all our hard work and all of our successes. But what choice do we have, Lee? What else *can* we do?"

"Not air our dirty laundry in front of these kids," he said.

"These *kids* are trying to destroy our facility!" Mary Ellen argued. "And they just might succeed!"

"What if you disable the surveillance system?" Daphne suggested.

"We need that system to monitor our patients," Lee replied. "It's not just about broadcasting to the subscribers but making sure the operations run smoothly."

"Can you stop broadcasting to the subscribers?" Brock suggested.

"That wouldn't be enough," Mary Ellen said. "Many of them watch in person, right here on the island, and participate in the games."

"We could tell them all to go to hell if our number one fan didn't own this resort and most of the island," Lee said through a clenched jaw.

Daphne gawked. "Arturo Gomez?"

The two doctors exchanged looks. Now Daphne understood. The bloodline of this resort came from a watcher.

"Can't he be reasoned with?" Brock released Dr. Reynolds.

Daphne crossed her arms. "I'm sure they've tried."

"Like I said, the watchers don't just watch," Mary Ellen said. "They enter the games. It's Dr. Gray's concept of living art—her greatest ambition was to see this happen—and it's a great thrill to Arturo and to the others. Some have moved out to the island and have made living art their new lifestyle."

"It's better than any other interactive game," Lee added. "Better than Dungeons and Dragons. Better than video games."

"It makes them feel alive because their world is boring or painful, otherwise," Mary Ellen continued. "So they consume thrilling story after story so they can ignore the reality of their lives. The more real the stories feel, the more easily they can deceive themselves into avoiding real life. The art becomes their real life, if that makes any sense."

"This was not what Dr. Gray anticipated," Lee said.

"And they make unreasonable demands," Mary Ellen continued. "If our exercises become boring to them, or if they disagree with their value, they complain and pull back their support. We're no longer free to practice as we see fit."

"It makes us compromise our work," Lee explained. "And we've managed to create a terrible addiction that we continually feed, because our real patients depend on it."

"Both the science and the art are being undermined by consumerism," Mary Ellen said.

Suddenly they heard more than one set of footsteps coming from Hortense Gray's office.

"I didn't get to tell them the most important thing," Mary Ellen said as she quickly returned the switches to their positions and led the teens back into her office.

Just before the door closed, they heard Hortense Gray say, "We're getting complaints. Has something happened?"

"A momentary glitch in the system," Lee said. "We might need Vince and Dave to come take a look at it."

"Get them on it right away," Arturo demanded.

Shaking from the close call, Daphne studied Mary Ellen Rose. What if all she had said was just part of another exercise? "What were you going to say? What's the most important thing?" She wanted so badly to ask if it had anything to do with Emma, but she bit her tongue, because she didn't want to get Greg in trouble, if he was telling the truth. Also, she wasn't sure she'd believe Mary Ellen, anyway.

Mary Ellen smiled and said, "Just that you understand this really is a war, right? A war against suicide."

Daphne turned to Brock, feeling more confused than ever.

CHAPTER TWELVE

Goodbye at Prisoners Harbor

Once Daphne and Brock were back in his unit, she led him to the bathroom and closed the door, locking it. Then she turned on the shower.

The first thing she did was check the drawer for the journal. It was still there! She opened it and took pictures of several of the pages.

"Good thinking," Brock said.

"Guess what!" She turned to face him when she'd got all the shots she wanted. "I recorded everything Mary Ellen said on my phone."

"Really?"

"Let's make sure it turned out. It would suck royally if it didn't."

Daphne clicked on the video. It showed mostly the inside of her short's pocket, but, sure enough, they could hear their conversation with Mary Ellen perfectly. They listened all the way to the end. Daphne was pleased to have also gotten their conversation in the surveillance room, especially the part about the investors putting Emma's life in terrible jeopardy.

"Too bad we couldn't get them to say Emma was murdered," Brock said.

"It doesn't matter. We'll show this to the police officer on the boat from Prisoners Harbor," Daphne said gleefully. "Then he'll have no choice but to radio for reinforcements. Don't you think? Don't you think that's enough?"

"Maybe. But what if that was…"

"Just another game?"

"Yeah." Brock took her in his arms.

"She knows I want to go to the police," Daphne said. "So she told me all those things hoping to change my mind, to get me to feel sorry for her."

"Did it work?"

"What if she's telling the truth?"

He shrugged.

"I do feel bad, in a way. Don't you? I mean, this place really helped me. If we can get them out here, the FBI will probably arrest Dr. Gray and the others. Maybe even Cam."

"Let's just put this in their hands. You've done enough."

The last thing Daphne wanted was to see Cam—or any of the Calibans—go to jail. Maybe she needed to rethink her strategy.

The jeep ride to Prisoners Harbor was quiet. Daphne rode in the front beside Roger, and Brock was in the back with the police officer. When they reached the pier, they found Cam and his mother saying goodbye. Brock carried Daphne's pack (she carried his lighter overnight bag) and walked past them to the boat, and the police officer followed, but Daphne waited by Cam, whose back was to her as he was hugging his mother goodbye. His mother's face was full of tears, and she was shaking.

"Please, Cameron," Mrs. Turner said desperately. "Just come home for a visit. You can always come back."

"I will," he said. "I promise. But now isn't a good time."

"As long as I know you're coming. Maybe this summer?"

"Maybe so."

Mrs. Turner hugged her son one more time and went to the boat.

"Cam?" Daphne said as adrenaline pumped through her. She prayed he wouldn't ignore her again.

He turned and looked down at her, frowning. "Hey, Daphne."

She sighed with relief. At least he was speaking to her.

"I'm so sorry," she said.

"I know you are. Just give me some time."

"What if I chose *you*?" She was shocked by the words spilling from her mouth. "Would you come home with us, then?"

"How can you be so cruel?"

She wanted to tell him that she really did love him, and that she had always loved him. Tear pricked her eyes. It would only hurt him more to hear it, so she bit her lip and said nothing.

Cam gazed into her eyes with a tortured expression on his face. Then before she knew what was happening, he pulled her lips to his and pressed his mouth hard against them. The touch was a mixture of passion and anger, and it left Daphne breathless.

Dazed and with a face full of heat, she said nothing more as she carried Brock's overnight bag across her shoulder and boarded the boat. She could see Brock gawking in her peripheral vision, but she wouldn't look at him, afraid of what her own face might betray.

She broke into tears as they headed away from Prisoners Harbor, because she knew she needed to talk to the officer and expose the resort, but another part of her felt so grateful for what it had done for her and her family, that she felt like showing the officer would be a betrayal, not just to Dr. Gray, but to Cam and to all of the Calibans.

By the time they reached Scorpion Anchorage to pick up a few of the campers heading back to the mainland, Daphne had a panicky feeling that she was letting Cam down by leaving without him. She had an equally panicky feeling that talking to the police officer and the FBI would cause more harm than good.

She hefted her pack from the floor of the boat and strapped it on.

"What are you doing?" Brock asked, alarmed.

"I can't leave," she said. "I have too many unanswered questions. I've got to stay and figure things out."

"Let the cops do that."

"I can't. I'm so sorry, Brock. This is something that I have to do."

"I can't afford to stay. I have that meet. My scholarship depends on it."

"I know."

"Please don't do this. I'll be worried sick." Brock closed his eyes and shook his head. When he opened them again, they were moist. "I know you feel sorry for them, but they're not children. They're old enough to decide for themselves. They're the ones pushing the buttons and pulling the strings. Why should you risk your neck for them?"

"Because they did save me, and they saved Joey." Tears tumbled down her cheeks. "And because now I want to save them back."

"You're in love with him, aren't you?" Brock accused, as another wave of tears rushed to his eyes.

"No," she said, though inside she knew that wasn't completely true. "And this isn't about my feelings. It's about doing the right thing."

Mrs. Turner noticed Daphne crying and asked what was wrong.

"I just can't leave," Daphne said. "I need answers."

"Good. Then I'll stay, too," Mrs. Turner said.

Daphne wasn't sure if that was a good idea, but she honestly needed a friend she could trust.

Brock cupped Daphne's face and said, "Tell me I'm not losing you."

"You aren't losing me," she said, as more tears tumbled down her face. She hoped she had convinced him more than she'd manage to convince herself.

When she and Mrs. Turner were alone on the pier watching the catamaran head back to the mainland, Daphne asked, "Do you think we're doing the right thing?"

"Do you feel anxious or relieved, dear?"

She thought about that. The panicky feeling had gone away. "Relieved."

"Me, too," Mrs. Turner said. "That means we're doing the right thing."

The sun was about to set by the time another boat came, and the wind was chilly. There was no one waiting for them at Prisoners Harbor, so they hiked along the canyon ridge for half an hour before the bright lights of the resort came into view. During that time, Daphne warned Mrs. Turner about the cameras.

"They're everywhere, except in the restrooms," she said. "They even have them out on the beach and out in Central Valley."

"That's a bit excessive."

"Just don't say anything you don't want overheard."

Whatever was coming, Daphne was glad to be there. She wanted more answers, which she would never get back home. Her heart pumping, she and Mrs. Turner descended into the canyon.

CHAPTER THIRTEEN

An Unexpected Welcome

As Daphne and Mrs. Turner followed the sidewalk into the resort, someone rushed from the doors of the main building and ran up the sidewalk toward them. Daphne couldn't tell who it was at first in the dark of evening, but once he was about fifty feet away, his identity was unmistakable.

It was Cam.

"You came back!" he shouted, happily.

Daphne and Mrs. Turner exchanged looks of confusion.

"I didn't think you would!" he cried out as he got closer. "Dr. Gray and Dr. Rose nailed it. I can't believe it!"

As soon as he reached them, he hugged his mom and then lifted Daphne—backpack and all—into the air. Cam lost his footing from the weight and they both fell back on their bottoms, Cam laughing with glee.

"I can't believe you came back!" He jumped to his feet and whisked Daphne in his arms, her pack remaining in a heap on the sidewalk. "You passed the test." He pointed to the sky. "You see that? She passed the test!"

Daphne realized he was pointing to the cameras and talking to the watchers.

"Now you get to come with me to the planning room," he said.

"Cameron, what in the world are you talking about?" his mother asked when Daphne couldn't speak.

Daphne was utterly bewildered.

Cam set Daphne down on her feet and put an arm around his mother's neck. "Don't you worry about a thing, Mom. You just go get yourself checked in. They'll put you back in the same unit. And Daphne will be just on the other side, in twelve, where Brock was. I'll meet you in an hour for dinner. Come on."

He picked up Daphne's pack and carried it as they continued to the main building. When they entered the lobby, a crowd of the regulars were there waiting with smiles and applause.

"Welcome back!" Stan called.

"Way to go, Daphne!" Dave said.

"Oh, my God." Greg rushed up and gave her a hug. "I'm so relieved. I feel like everything was my fault."

Daphne was at a loss. She had no idea what in the heck was going on.

As someone helped Mrs. Turner check in at the front desk, Daphne was whisked into the elevator.

"What's happening?" she finally asked, once she and most of the younger crowd were in the elevator going up. She didn't even have time to be afraid or anxious about the elevator; she was too freaked out by everyone's mysterious behavior.

"You've made it to the next level, kiddo," Stan explained with a wink. "The fact that you came back, in spite of everything you were led to believe, means you are dedicated to our mission, whether you know it or not."

"That makes you a planner," Cam said. "Like us."

Holy moly. They wanted to make her a Caliban?

Still dazed, she followed them from the elevator onto the second floor, where they passed all three doctors' offices and took a turn down another long corridor.

At the end of it, Stan opened the double doors, saying "Welcome to the planning room."

Inside was a conference room, and waiting for them, already seated at each end of a long table, were Doctors Rose and Gray.

"Come in, Daphne, and have a seat," Hortense Gray said with a smile.

"Welcome, hon," Dr. Rose said. "I'm so relieved you came back."

The regulars began seating themselves at the table. Stan, Vince, and Dave went around to the opposite side, and Greg took a chair next to his mother.

"I don't understand what's going on," Daphne said. She glanced to the walls at what appeared to be story boards—charcoal sketches of the shark attack, the high tide at the sea cave, the elevator drop, and other images, not all familiar to her.

Cam moved to a seat beside Dr. Rose and pointed out a chair beside him for Daphne. "Have a seat."

Daphne was still processing everything around her and was too bewildered to sit.

"You've been invited into the highest tier of our facility," Dr. Gray explained. "We are the creative ones who come up with the stories we use to treat our patients and our viewers. It's one of the few places where there is no surveillance."

"Sit down," Cam said, pulling out the chair for her. "I still can't believe she came back. You ladies really nailed it."

The two doctors smiled.

"We were counting on it," Dr. Gray said.

"Praying for it is more accurate," Dr. Rose said.

Greg shook his head and leaned toward Daphne over the empty chair between them. "I'm sorry, Daphne. You wouldn't be here trying to destroy this place if it weren't for me, but I didn't know."

"I didn't know either, cuz," Vince, directly across from Greg, said. "I was about to run away with you."

"You wouldn't." Dave punched Vince in the arm.

"I came close. You were fooled, too. She had us all fooled." Vince glanced quickly at Dr. Gray and then averted his eyes.

"Except for me," Stan said. "I was in on the planning."

"They're talking about Emma," Cam explained.

"What?" Her heart skipped a beat. "Does that mean…" Daphne couldn't finish her question.

"Can I bring her out now?" Greg asked his mom.

Dr. Gray nodded.

Greg jumped up and went to a door across the room. He opened it, and in walked Emma.

Daphne's jaw dropped open. She stared at Emma, scanning her from head to toe. Was it really her? Or did she have a twin? Everyone in the room laughed at her reaction, and she was dizzy, and the room was spinning.

"I was the same way," Cam reassured her. "But it's true. It's really her."

Emma walked around the room to Daphne's side of the table and held out her arms. "Can I have a hug?"

Daphne stood up on weak, trembling knees and hugged the girl she'd believed to be dead.

When she sat back down at the table between Cam and Emma, Daphne put her head down on the table and sobbed. The laughter and smiles around the table were immediately subdued. Emma patted Daphne's back, and Cam rubbed her arm.

Daphne narrowed her eyes at Cam. "Why didn't you tell me at Scorpion Valley?"

"I couldn't risk you saying something in front of the watchers."

She wiped the tears from her cheeks. "That was a mean trick."

"But it was a necessary one," Dr. Gray said. "Allow me to explain."

"Why should I believe anything you say?" Daphne managed to choke out.

"This is the truth room, kiddo," Stan said. "Only the truth is allowed to be spoken here."

"Yeah, right," Daphne complained. Like any of them cared anything about the truth.

"Just hear her out," Cam said softly.

"I'm sorry," Emma said. "It wasn't my idea, but I'm sorry just the same."

"I'm going to start from the beginning," Hortense said. "And explain to you how this compound came to be."

"Here we go again," Dave snickered, but one look from Dr. Gray silenced him.

"During my studies as an undergrad at Princeton, I became very interested in a theory of Freud's about the connection between art and childhood play," Hortense began. "Freud wrote that children derive immense pleasure from their play—from their pretending. I know that during my days at the orphanage, the other children and I used to play 'cowboys and Indians.' That wouldn't be politically correct today, but, back then, we didn't know better. All the black children were made by the white to take the role of Indians. What the other children didn't know was that I quite enjoyed playing the Indian. I imagined having beautiful feathers on my head and colorful paint on my face. I pretended to carry an elegant bow and arrow and imagined that I had power, which was so opposite my circumstances that it took quite a lot of imagining. I took good care of my pretend horse, riding and feeding her regularly. It was an intense life out there on the playground, and all this pretending seemed very real to us orphans.

"Once I was adopted, my adopted siblings and I would pretend to be psychologists, like our father. We didn't get to go outside and play together for more than a few minutes each day, but just like it had been at the orphanage, our playtime was intense. We didn't always play psychologists. One boy invented a game of little people and giants. Another pretended to be an explorer. Oh, we also played like we were on the *Star Trek Enterprise.*"

Several of the regulars laughed.

"As a psychology student, I was enthralled by Freud's idea that because play brings us such immense pleasure as children, we do not want to let go of it as adults. He theorized that because it isn't acceptable for adults to continue their play, they find a replacement for that source of pleasure, and that replacement is art.

"Art is the socially acceptable way for adults to derive pleasure from pretending. Freud wrote that the fiction writer is the best example. The writer of fiction is like the one child on the playground who creates the imaginary world, and the readers of fiction are like the kids who go along with the game, sometimes amending it as they play by offering suggestions.

"I noticed, as I contemplated Freud's teachings, that most of our very best stories provide a cathartic experience for readers. They put us through an emotional journey that leaves us feeling reborn and revitalized by the end. I began reading other thinkers who talked about the cathartic power of art, like Nietzsche's *The Birth of Tragedy.*

"By the time I became a graduate student at Harvard, I had already developed my concept of living art as a form of therapy. It seemed to me that if a story could provide a life-changing experience for readers, then jumping into the pages of the book would be that much more intense. Patients who suffer from clinical depression could benefit from an opportunity to go back to childhood play, so that they could live the art more intensely than a normal reader.

"I began by turning part of the basement of my building at Harvard into a laboratory for experimenting with adult play—what I quickly named 'living art' so as not to be confused with anything sexual. Like a child on a playground, I created games and scenarios, and I soon found that the games that put the subjects through a terrifying experience had the best outcomes, especially when the subject was led to believe that the experience was real. Although knowing that a game was *just a game* still managed to bring great pleasure to my subjects, the belief that a game was *real* brought an even higher level of catharsis to my subjects.

"My elevator exercise, like the one you underwent here, Daphne, began in that building at Harvard. That exercise, more than any other up to that point, brought my subjects a profound cathartic experience. At the end of it, many of them shouted for joy and kissed the floor and said how grateful they were to be alive. I felt I was onto something important.

"Around that time, I met Mary Ellen, a fellow grad student, and she joined me in developing our experimental exercises.

"As our therapeutic games became more and more elaborate, the basement at Harvard became too small. We were eventually allowed the use of an entire building on weekends to conduct our research. This building had a ballroom and over a dozen meeting rooms on multiple levels. Although not every experiment concluded with a positive result, the experience was overall a great success and crucial to our research.

"Not long after I finished my doctoral studies at Harvard, I left my teaching post to pursue my therapeutic exercises as a practitioner. I went from one location to another, but had difficulty finding the ideal facility.

"A few years after I left Harvard, I became pregnant with Gregory and my ambitions came to a halt. His father and I had broken up before I knew of the pregnancy, and I had to raise him as a single parent. It was at that time that I joined Lee Reynolds in his behavioral studies at Cornell. Lee was adopted by my father from the same orphanage at the same time I was, and so we had spent five years together at Madam Wesslock's together, and then another six or seven years together in the same household, until Lee ran away. That's a story for another time. Anyway, we reconnected at my father's funeral and, afterward, kept in touch, so when I found myself in need of a job as a single mother, he helped me out."

Daphne let that sink in: Lee Reynolds was Dr. Gray's adoptive brother.

"By the time Gregory was seven, I had tracked down his father, and we reunited, though we never married. He was enthralled with my concept of living art and happened to be terribly wealthy, so together we sought a property to build our treatment center. After a few failed attempts on the mainland, we finally began the development of this facility out here on Santa Cruz Island, and both Lee and Mary Ellen were thrilled when I invited them to join me. Arturo had become very involved in the conservation movement and saw an opportunity to help save this island from years of neglect, to rid it of invasive and non-native species and to save the endemic plants and wildlife from extinction. By moving out here, he was able to combine his passion for conservation with his growing obsession with my living art.

"For ten years, we have built this place into the magnificent and successful center you and your family have had the benefit of experiencing. We have healed countless lives that were devastated by loss, grief, guilt, post-traumatic stress disorder, and a number of mental illnesses. Early on, we recruited subscribers, also called watchers, who had either already undergone their own treatment with us or who simply relished the intense experience of play. We, of course, targeted people with large amounts of disposable income who could continue to provide us with a stable cash flow for our often elaborate needs. And we've shared a cooperative and symbiotic relationship with the subscribers until recently.

"You've already met many of them. In addition to Arturo Gomez, we have Phillip Johnson, Pete Wellington, Roger Huggins, Marty Evers, and Kelly Mangold participating regularly here on the island, though Pete only comes for the summers. We also have others on the mainland making trips out here a few times a year for major games, like our annual ballroom exercise. Several subscribers have never set foot on the island but like to watch our private channel, a live stream they access with a password.

"Our problem is that once a subscriber joins us, he or she rarely wishes to discontinue. The pleasure we provide is like no other, and so unless a major change in their circumstances prevents them from fulfilling their financial obligations to us, our watchers tend to stick with us indefinitely. We, at first, found this to be a positive consequence, because we came to a point where we no longer needed to invest our time and energy in recruiting subscribers. But over the past few years, we've come to realize the devastatingly negative consequence: our subscribers have become bored.

"You see, those of us who are planners are more concerned with the healing and transformation of our patients, and so we receive pleasure and satisfaction from each and every one of our successes; however, the watchers, who are involved primarily for the pleasure of play, become tired of watching the same exercises over and over, even though the exercises have infinite variations because of the differing personalities of our subjects. In the past few years, some of the subscribers have put a lot of pressure on us to take more risks and to put our patients through evermore frightening exercises. Because I have seen our successes continue, I have allowed it. And the fact that Arturo, our major investor, is one of the most ardent supporters of greater risk and more variation, well, we felt we had no choice.

"The exercise with Emma was my attempt to teach the watchers a lesson. I at first believed the gunshots alone would show them the danger of their requests. Unfortunately, Arturo experienced a tremendous high from the near-death experience of Emma, and that whole exercise backfired on me. That's when Dr. Rose and I had the idea of staging a death.

"We were afraid that if too many planners were in on this exercise, we wouldn't be able to fool the watchers, so only Stan, Mary Ellen, and Lee and I knew what was going one. And Emma, of course. We needed her to agree to 'slip and fall.' We needed Stan for his scuba diving skills.

He was also needed to dye her body with blue and black ink and to paint her lips and eyelids blue.

"To motivate Greg to want to leave the island with Emma, I pretended to disapprove of their relationship. Emma didn't know I was pretending. In fact, I used my apparent disapproval to solicit her cooperation every step of the way. Because I loved her like a daughter, and I believed she loved me, I felt our relationship could withstand this deceit and she would eventually forgive me.

"And by the way, she was full of anesthetics during the ballroom scene. She suffered no pain when she was shot. I know not everyone will agree that the risk was worth taking, but I had hired a well-decorated marksman for accuracy. I would never put my Emma in any *real* harm's way."

"That's why I was a blubbering mess," Emma said. "The medications made me loopy and emotional."

"Narcotics will do that to you," Hortense said.

"Good thing, too, because I thought the gunman was going to be a lot closer when he pulled the trigger," Emma said. "If I'd known he was going to shoot at me from that distance, well…"

"Anyway," Hortense continued. "I counted on Greg's reaction to Emma's death to engage the watchers, and I wasn't disappointed; but what I didn't anticipate was Greg's renewed desire to leave me and the island and his ability to succeed. After months of trying to track him down, I finally found him shortly after he contacted you. I had always planned to tell him the truth about Emma within a few days of the event, but his leaving made that impossible. Then, when we learned he had begged you to involve the FBI, well, we feared our facility was in danger of scrutiny, and we doubted it would survive an investigation.

"When a month or two passed by, and we saw no sign of your return, we thought we were in the clear. Then you showed up a few days ago, and we've been on high alert ever since."

"I'm so sorry," Greg said again.

Hortense turned to her son. "You need to stop that right now, Gregory. You have nothing to feel sorry about. In fact, that scare with Daphne is what inspired me to come up with a solution."

Greg nodded as his face turned red.

Hortense looked across the table at Daphne. "Before your arrival, we were in the process of planning another of what we've come to call a 'grand finale.' In fact, Giovanni overheard, and he ran away before allowing us a chance to explain. This upset me a great deal, because I was in the process of adopting him and making him a permanent member of our family here on the island. I hope to eventually find him again. Maybe he will come back on his own."

Daphne was surprised to see something she rarely saw in Dr. Gray: emotion. Hortense collected herself and then continued.

"Your decision to come back, Daphne, means that you still feel gratitude and loyalty to this facility, which is good because we need your help. We need you to help us drive away our subscribers—even Arturo Gomez."

Daphne's mouth dropped open.

Greg said, "I'm giving my mom my trust fund, so she can start again."

Hortense smiled at her son and squeezed his hand. "You see, both Philip and Marty have threatened to blackmail me. They'll turn me over to the authorities if I don't allow them to stay and continue to play in the games—that's how addicted they've become. And, of course, they want the games to be much too risky."

"But how are you going to drive them all away?" Daphne asked.

"We have a plan," Hortense Gray said.

"That's why we're so glad you came back, hon," Dr. Rose said. "You can help us better than anyone."

"It's getting late." Dr. Gray stood up. "I know everyone is hungry for dinner. So let's call it a night. We'll reconvene tomorrow after breakfast, at ten o'clock."

As they were about to leave the planning room to head for the dining hall upstairs, Greg stopped Daphne by taking her arm. He glanced around at the others, already on their way out, and then leaned in and whispered, "Just in case you're curious, Lee was subject number six."

Daphne covered her mouth. Subject number six was mentioned at least a dozen times in Malcom's journal about Hortense. She wondered if the journal remained in the bathroom drawer of Brock's unit, or if it had been discovered and removed. She tried not to get her hopes up as she followed the others upstairs for dinner, still teeming with all she'd just heard.

CHAPTER FOURTEEN

Subject Number Six

Dazed and quiet, Daphne was still trying to process everything she'd been told and could barely eat at dinner. She and Mrs. Turner sat with Cam at a table with the younger crowd. Bridget was still not among them. Emma, too, was absent. She wasn't allowed outside of her suite, because the subscribers couldn't know she was alive. How much longer would she have to live like a prisoner?

Greg's final comment to her before they had left the planning room was also weighing on Daphne's mind. So, if Lee was, at least for a time, Hortense's adoptive brother, then was his affection for her mere brotherly love? Cam had told her last summer that he thought Lee was in love with Hortense. If Lee had run away and taken a different last name, maybe his love for her was one of the reasons he left Malcolm Gray— not that he needed another reason.

Also, Daphne had heard Vince refer to Greg as "cuz" more than once, but she hadn't thought anything of it. Did they consider themselves cousins?

Daphne wondered about Vince's mom, too. Lee barely acknowledged his son. Maybe he'd never learned how to be a father, since he didn't really have one himself.

It seemed to Daphne that even the behavior of the most brilliant psychologists was subject to forces outside of their control. No amount of college credit or research could teach them how to be better and more loving parents.

Across the room, three new people, whom Daphne had never met, entered, but after what she'd been told, she had a feeling the man, woman, and teen were Toni and her parents. Toni wore a scarf around what was likely a bald head. She was the one Giovanni had said was transitioning from a boy to a girl, because she felt like a girl trapped in a boy's body. Giovanni had also said that Toni had given the doctors the bucket. Daphne wondered what else, if anything, the doctors had in store for her and her parents.

None of them looked very happy right now as they filled their trays with food at the buffet line.

"You okay?" Cam asked, interrupting her thoughts.

Things were still awkward and tense between them. "Not sure."

"Remember, everything that happens in the planning room stays in the planning room," he added.

She'd been told that several times on the way up from the second floor. "I know."

"You're not eating very much," he said.

"Yeah. I'm not that hungry."

"Want me to walk you back to your room?"

"That'd be great."

Cam's mom, who seemed happy to be spending more time with her son, joined them as they made their way from the main building back toward the cabanas.

"I'm sorry about Dad," Cam said to her.

She waved her hand in a dismissive gesture. "Oh, honey, that was a long time ago."

"No, I mean Fred," Cam said.

Mrs. Turner covered her smile. "Oh."

Daphne and Cam exchanged glances.

"It's no sweat off my back, really," Mrs. Turner said. "I never loved Fred like I loved your real father."

"I didn't know that," Cam said.

Fred had been more like a father to Cam than his biological one had. Fred was the one that Cam had loved, as far as Daphne knew.

"It's why I never changed my name," Mrs. Turner said.

Cam draped an arm across his mom's shoulders. "But you always said it was so that our names would be the same."

"That was one reason." She stopped and looked up at him beneath the full moon. "But the truth is your father—and I mean Carl—was the one great love of my life."

"He was?" Cam asked.

"They say some people get more than one, and some never find it at all; but the majority of us get one great love in our lives, and Carl was it. He broke my heart."

"Then why did you marry Fred?" Cam asked.

"Because I knew he'd be a good father to you. And he was."

A tear glistened on Mrs. Turner's cheek as she turned and continued along the sidewalk. Cam pulled her in close to him as they walked side by side. Daphne walked alongside Cam, wishing she wasn't there, so they could have their moment.

They stopped at Mrs. Turner's unit. Daphne wondered if she should say her goodbyes here, but Cam hugged his mom and said goodnight before Daphne could decide what to do.

"See you at breakfast," he said.

"Goodnight, sweet boy," Mrs. Turner said. "It's such a pleasure to be in your company. I'm so grateful to Daphne."

Daphne smiled. "I'm glad to be here, too. Good night, Mrs. Turner."

They waited as she entered her unit, closing the door behind her, and then they went around the building to Daphne's side.

"So are we friends again?" Daphne asked him as they reached her door.

He cleared his throat and turned red in the face. "You hurt me pretty bad—I won't lie. But I've never stopped being your friend."

She smiled, full of relief. "Wanna come in for a while?" She really didn't want to be alone.

He hesitated, and she almost thought he'd say no, when he surprised her with a nod. "Sure."

"I just need to use the bathroom," she said once they were inside.

The first thing she did was check the drawer where she had left Malcolm Gray's journal. She gasped with excitement when she found it still there. She was anxious to read it and had quite a lot of things she wanted to ask Cam, but she couldn't in front of the cameras. She needed to get him to come into the bathroom with her.

How awkward.

They'd been friends for a long time. Surely their relationship could handle a little pretending.

She closed the drawer with the journal inside, did her business, and went back out to Cam.

He'd already turned on the television and was searching for something to watch.

"Hey, Cam?"

"Yeah?"

"How would you feel about, um, taking a shower?" her face was red hot, and as soon as the words were out of her mouth, she wished she could take them back. She really thought she could be a better actress than this.

He laughed, keeping his eyes on the television. "What, with you?"

When he looked at her, she winked, trying to signal to him what she really meant, but obviously she was sending the wrong signal because his expression was raw shock.

He shook his head and took a few steps back, clutching the remote between them like a weapon. "What are you asking me?"

"Just as friends." Awkwardly, she added, "With benefits."

"I, uh…"

She sighed and rolled her eyes.

"I can't," he said, wiping beads of sweat from his forehead. "Maybe I should go."

She didn't want things to end this way. She needed to let him know what she was really trying to do.

"Okay," she said. "But before you go, would you mind taking a look at the toilet? I don't think it's flushing properly."

His expression changed, and it was as if a light had gone off inside his head. "Sure."

He followed her into the bathroom.

"Geez, Louise," she said locking the door behind them.

He lifted his hands in frustration. "Why couldn't you have just asked about the toilet in the first place?"

"I didn't think of it."

Suddenly he met her eyes with the glare of a wolf. Before she could take another breath, he pressed her against the bathroom door, pinning her with his body, and slammed his lips hard against hers.

A whirlwind of emotions swept through her, and even though she *shouldn't* keep kissing him back, she *loved* kissing him back, and *wanted* to keep kissing him back, and had never *wanted him so badly*.

"Cam," she breathed.

He stepped back and leaned his hands on his knees, panting. "I'm sorry."

She wasn't sorry, but she stopped herself from admitting it. It would be wrong to move forward with Cam without first breaking things off with Brock, and she still hadn't decided if that's what she should do. What was she thinking? Of course, she didn't want to break up with Brock…did she? As much as she longed to keep kissing Cam, she had to be strong.

There were more important things going on right now.

The journal.

"It's okay," she said, coming down from the high. "You're an amazing kisser. Even for a *Star Wars* geek."

He shook his head. "You ain't seen nothin' yet."

Her heart fluttered at the thought of kissing him again, but she cleared her head and said, "I need to show you something."

She turned on the shower, which made him gawk, but before he could say anything, she opened the drawer and handed him the journal.

"What's this?" he asked.

"Greg gave it to me. It's Malcolm Gray's journal on subject seven."

"Subject seven?" He flipped open to the first page.

"Hortense Gray."

"Oh, my God." He slid onto the floor with his back to the vanity, absorbing the first few pages, just as she had.

She sat beside him. "I guess you've never seen this before?"

"Nuh-uh."

"Greg told me tonight that Lee Reynolds was subject number six."

Cam looked up at her, horrified. "No wonder."

"What's the deal with Vince's mom, anyway?"

"She died about four years ago," Cam said.

"Oh."

"Vince grew up with her and didn't have anything to do with his father before then."

"So he and his dad never got close?"

"Dr. Gray put them through therapy, and that helped them some, but neither one of them seems that interested."

"It's up to the father to make an effort," she said. "It shouldn't be on Vince."

Cam turned to the next page of the journal. "Every once in a while, there's mention of subject number six. Like right here, on the second page:

"Still reeling from the tantrum I endured from Subject No. Six…"

"I saw that." She took the journal and turned to a few pages in. "There's also this one:"

"*Hortense showed concern over the gashes on my face made by Subject No. Six...*"

"Way to go, Lee," Cam said.

"So you agree that Malcom was a monster, right?" she asked, not sure how brainwashed he was. "Pain can never be an acceptable form of treatment. You get that, right?"

"Of course. Geez," he said, shaking his head. "Even Dr. Gray says so."

Daphne arched a brow.

"Seriously. She said it brings pleasure, but not healing."

Pleasure? That sounded pretty sick. "So you still support what she does here?"

"Now that I know what the watchers have been doing to us." He looked back at the journal. "But how can Dr. Gray say that her father was a great man?"

Daphne shrugged. "Maybe she wants to believe that her suffering meant something."

"And that her father loved her," Cam added. "I know what that's like."

Daphne squeezed his arm, and they turned back to the journal.

"Oh, look at this," Daphne said, pointing to the top of the next page.

June 2, 1982

Subject No. 7

As noted in my records of Subject No. Six, I caught Six and Seven in a lover's embrace on one of the park benches in my back garden. I observed them for a few minutes, surprised that of all the boys I've brought here, Hortense would choose the scrawniest among them.

In most of the scholarship I've studied, females tend to choose those males with the most likely survival rate. This usually translates into males of bulk, beauty, and, sometimes, wit. Subject No. Six exhibits none of those traits, though admittedly, his anger and rage toward me might hinder their manifestations. When I questioned Hortense about the matter in the garden, her black face turned red.

I asked her if she liked Subject No. Six.

She said she liked that he paid attention to her.

I asked her if she considered him her brother.

She said she used to, but not anymore.

When I asked her what had changed, she asked if I would speak of something else.

"I guess that answers my question," Daphne said. She wondered if there still existed anything between them.

Cam crossed one leg over the other. "I wonder if Vince knows."

"Oh, look here, a few pages over." Daphne pointed again.

August 13, 1982

Subject No. 7

Hortense is still despondent over the loss of Subject No. 6. The rest of the household seems better for it, but she exhibits clear signs of depression.

I told her that her mood would improve once she resumed school.

Then she surprised me by asking for a treatment. She lay on her belly across her bed and lifted her shirt. Unlike the other subjects, I hadn't treated her since she began the private schooling two years ago, but I did as she requested. I took my belt and administered three whips. As in the past, she flinched but did not cry out.

When I had finished, I asked if the treatments comforted her.

She said they did not.

I asked why she had requested them, if they didn't bring her comfort.

She said she needed to recall why Lee (Subject No. Six) ran away.

Daphne looked up at Cam. "That's so…heartbreaking."

"Yeah."

They were interrupted by a loud pounding on the exterior door.

Daphne turned off the shower. "Is that someone knocking?"

"I'll check." Cam jumped up off the floor and went to the front door.

Daphne tucked the journal away in its drawer and followed.

It was Stan. "Sorry to interrupt."

He looked back and forth at them, and Daphne suddenly realized why. He had expected them to be wet from the shower.

"What's up?" Cam asked.

"Hortense wants us to draw your mom into an exercise, to help her deal with the loss of your dad," Stan said.

Daphne was surprised to see Cam frown.

"I think she's over Fred," Cam said.

"Not Fred. Carl."

Cam crossed his arms over his chest. "My mom underwent therapy two summers ago."

"Dr. Gray believes your mom needs more help."

"What does she have in mind?" Daphne asked.

"I'm glad you asked," Stan said. "Because it involves you."

CHAPTER FIFTEEN

Coma

Beneath the full moon, Daphne went around her building to Mrs. Turner's door and took a deep breath. Here we go again, she thought. Did she have it in her to do this? And, even if she did, should she?

She had to admit, it *was* thrilling. And maybe it really *would* help Cam's mom.

Resolved, she pounded on the door. "Mrs. Turner? Mrs. Turner, wake up! Please!" After a moment, she pounded again. "Mrs. Turner?"

In another moment, Cam's mom opened the door in her nightgown and robe. "What is it, Daphne?"

"Cam's been taken to the infirmary. He collapsed on the sidewalk outside my room."

The woman's face fell. "Well, my God. Let me throw some clothes on. Will you wait for me?"

"Of course."

"You want to come in and wait?"

"Sure."

Daphne sat on one of the chairs while Mrs. Turner went into the bathroom to change.

"When did this happen?" the woman asked through the cracked bathroom door.

"Just a few minutes ago. We were saying goodnight, and he, I don't know, *fainted.*"

"Dear, Lord. Did he hurt himself on the way down?"

"I don't know. I just freaked out and called the main building. They sent a couple of guys to carry him on a stretcher. He didn't come to, but he was breathing."

Mrs. Turner emerged from the bathroom, dressed. She had a peculiar look on her face. "Wait a minute."

"What's wrong?"

"I know what kind of place this is. Come on, Daphne. Cam didn't faint. This is one of those exercises, isn't it?"

Daphne frowned. "If it is, I'm fooled. Cam wasn't moving."

"If this is all a game, I'll be irked. Well, I guess I'd rather it was a game, but if it is, I'll be pretty darn irked."

"It seemed real to me."

"Let's not take any chances," she said, finding her shoes. "Let's go, dear."

They walked together in the quiet, chilly night past the swimming pool toward the main building and took the elevator up to the infirmary, where Stan was waiting outside the door.

"Philip says it might have been a stroke," Stan warned as they entered the reception area. "They have him in a room over here."

Even though she knew it was a game, the sight of Cam, stretched out in a hospital bed with an IV and other monitors hooked up to him, made her heart sink in her chest.

Philip stood on the other side of the bed, checking one of the monitors. "Oh, hello. Come on in."

"What's happened to him, Doctor?" Mrs. Turner asked, seeming alarmed for someone who hadn't believed moments ago.

"I'm waiting on some blood work to determine if it was a stroke or something else, like a seizure," Philip said. "Either way, he should have come out of it by now. He's still not responsive."

"You mean he's in a coma?" Daphne asked, as she had been instructed to do.

"I'm afraid so."

Mrs. Turner touched her son's cheek and stroked his hair. Daphne thought for sure it would make him flinch and give the game away, but Cam lay perfectly still.

Daphne moved beside Mrs. Turner and stared down at Cam. Now that his eyes were closed, she could study his features more closely, without him noticing. She knew his face better than her own, having watched it develop since they were small children. But his body had changed into something she hadn't been used to—something she had only noticed last summer when he had brought her to this place. She wouldn't admit it to herself then, because she had felt so bad for what she had done to Brock. And she loved Brock—*still* loved Brock, but now, now she allowed herself to realize how deeply she also loved Cam.

Maybe it was an even deeper, more mature love than what she felt for Brock, because its roots were deeper and older.

She touched Cam's arm and was astounded by how still he remained. He showed not the least bit reaction to the way his mother was combing her fingers through his hair, as though she were testing him. Daphne watched with growing anxiety as his mother's pats to his cheeks became slaps.

"Cameron Turner!" his mother cried. "Stop doing this to me!"

Stan moved between them and took Mrs. Turner's hands into his own. "I'm so sorry. I know this is hard."

The woman snapped around to face Stan. "Is this a game? Tell me the truth, son."

"I'm afraid his coma is real. I swear."

Stan lifted the lids of both of Cam's eyes at once. They were rolling in different directions!

Adrenaline raced through Daphne's body. "Oh my God!"

"Try to stay calm, Daphne. For Mrs. Turner's sake," Stan said.

Daphne struggled to maintain her composure as she began to suspect what was really going on. Had they induced a coma for the sake of the exercise? "Can I talk to you privately for a minute, Stan?"

They stepped from the room into the reception area. A woman sat behind the desk writing something down. Daphne took Stan out into the hallway, so they could be alone.

"What is going on?" she demanded. "Why isn't Cam responding?"

"Philip put him under, to make it more realistic for his mother."

Daphne wanted to scream. "You've got to be kidding me! Isn't that dangerous? Aren't there risks? What if he doesn't come out of it?"

"Apparently, doctors do this kind of thing all the time," Stan said.

"I want to talk to Philip," she said. "Where is he?"

"I…"

She didn't wait for Stan to answer. She stormed back into the reception area and asked the young woman behind the desk to please get the doctor there right away.

The woman picked up the phone and called him.

In a few minutes, Philip appeared in the reception room.

"You have no right to take such chances with human life," she said to him.

"I assure you, Cam is perfectly safe," Philip said calmly and quietly. "He's just under general anesthesia."

"Are you sure there aren't any risks?" she asked.

"Well, there's always some risk, but it's very small," he said.

Tears dropped onto her cheeks. "How small?"

"Maybe seven patients in every million die for unknown reasons while under."

Daphne relaxed a little but said, "He better not be one of them."

At that moment, Mrs. Turner walked into the reception area and noticed Daphne had been crying. The woman's eyes widened with fear and she gasped.

"It's real, isn't it?" Mrs. Turner said, nearly losing her step as she moved toward Daphne.

Philip caught her by the arm and steadied her. "I'm afraid so," he said. "In fact, I took the liberty of notifying Cam's father, and he's on his way to the island. He should be here by tomorrow evening."

Daphne and Mrs. Turner exchanged looks of surprise.

Mrs. Tuner raised her eyebrows at Philip. "Do you mean Fred? Or Carl?"

"Carl," Philip said. "According to my records, he is Cameron's biological father. Is that correct?"

Cam's mom turned, white faced, to Daphne, but was unable to say a word.

"Maybe you two should try to get some sleep," Philip said. "I'll call you if Cameron's condition changes."

"I don't think I can," Mrs. Turner said. "May I stay by his side?"

"Of course," Philip said.

Daphne went with Cam's mom back into the room where Cam lay as still as death. Only the subtle rise and fall of his chest indicated that he was alive.

<u>CHAPTER SIXTEEN</u>

The Plan

Sometime later, Daphne awoke and found herself hunched over in the chair in the room at the infirmary. Mrs. Turner was sound asleep in another chair beside her. Daphne got up and studied Cam's features—his slightly freckled cheeks, blond eyebrows, and peach lips. He remained unchanged since she'd last looked upon him.

"Oh, Cam," she whispered. "Please be okay. Please, please be okay. I meant it when I said I loved you. I really and truly did."

She wiped her eyes and looked at the time on her wristwatch. It was eight thirty in the morning. Wednesday morning. She decided she should go back to her room and shower and change. She had no clean clothes to change into, though, so she might need to borrow some from someone. She left the infirmary and went looking for Dr. Gray.

Stan met her in the hallway. "Hey, kiddo. You holding up all right?"

It was nice to see a friendly face. "I guess so."

Somehow Stan still had a way of making her feel better. He was like a big brother to her—like her own big brother: she wasn't always sure what she was going to get with him.

"Everybody else is still at breakfast," he said. "Want to grab some before the meeting?"

She'd forgotten about the planning meeting. "I'm not hungry, but I could use a change of clothes. Do you think you have anything I could borrow? I'd like to shower and change."

"I think I can help with that." He winked.

"Thanks."

"You sure do take a lot of showers," he teased.

Her face turned red as she followed him from the main building to his unit. He knew she hadn't really been in the shower, but whether he suspected she'd been making out with first Brock and then Cam, or whether he thought something closer to the truth, she didn't know.

As he rummaged through his drawers, she asked, "Do you think Cam will be okay?"

"I'm sure of it," he said. "Philip has done this before. It really is safe."

She sighed, feeling a bit more relieved, but she wouldn't feel completely at ease until Cam was up and talking.

"How's this?" Stan handed over a t-shirt and sweats.

"Perfect. Thanks." She'd been chilly all night in her shorts.

"See you at the meeting in half an hour?" he asked, as she headed toward his door.

"Sure." She reached for the knob.

"Hey, Daph?" he asked.

"Yeah?" She turned from the door to meet his eyes.

"This really isn't any of my business, but…" he paused. Maybe he was rethinking how to phrase his question.

"Spit it out."

"Are you having second thoughts about Brock?"

Heat rushed to her face. "You're right, Stan. It isn't any of your business. Now, if you'll excuse me…"

"I'm sorry. I shouldn't have asked. I just worry about you."

She nodded. "I get that. Thanks. See ya."

"See ya."

She rushed from Stan's unit toward her own, the adrenaline pounding through her veins. Boy, oh, boy, did she need that hot shower. Maybe it would help her forget the conflict deepening inside her heart.

After her shower, she dressed and took a walk up the boardwalk overlooking the beach. The wooden steps felt familiar beneath her boots, and when she reached the top, she glanced first toward the bluffs to her right—recalling the way she had dived from its peak—and then toward the hill of yellow poppies to her left before looking out to sea. She was once again surprised by the boats in the distance, because the resort made her feel like the island was isolated from the rest of civilization; but, civilization was out there, though more than a stone's throw away. Down below on the sand, Toni was raising her fists at her parents. Daphne wondered what was going on, but she turned away and headed for the infirmary to check on Cam.

Mrs. Turner was awake and staring fearfully at her son. When Daphne walked in, the woman looked up at her with red-rimmed eyes.

"You want to go get some breakfast?" Daphne asked.

Mrs. Turner shrugged. "I don't think I can eat."

"Maybe some hot coffee?"

"What if he wakes up?" she asked. "I want to be here when he does."

Daphne knew he wouldn't until the doctors decided to wake him up. "Then I'll bring some coffee back to you."

As she turned to go, Mrs. Turner said, "Daphne?"

Daphne stopped and faced Cam's mom.

"Most young people spend their lives looking forward to the future. They can't wait to grow up. They can't wait to go to college. They can't wait to get a career and maybe get married and start a family."

Daphne nodded. It had been true for her until Kara had died. Then things had changed.

"I was like that," Cam's mom continued. "But now I've learned that, if you live long enough, you arrive at a point in your life where all you do is reflect on the past. You wish you could go back and relive some parts of it and completely erase other parts of it. I'm at that point, I think. I don't have much to look forward to anymore."

"That's not true, Mrs. Turner."

"I don't know what I'm going to say to him."

Daphne stepped into the room and studied Cam. "Just tell him that you love him."

"What?" Mrs. Turner's face looked shocked. "No, dear. I'm talking about *Mr. Turner*, Cam's biological father."

"Oh."

"We saw each other here two summers ago, but I was still with Fred. I had Fred to lean on. This time, I'm all alone. I just don't think I can face him alone."

Daphne crossed the room and sat in the chair beside Cam's mom. "You're not alone. You have me. Okay?"

Mrs. Turner looked up at her with the hint of a smile and said, "Thank you, dear. I appreciate that. Just don't let me be alone in a room with him, if you can help it."

"He wasn't abusive, was he?"

"Oh, no. Not at all. I'm just worried I'll turn into the pathetic woman I was sixteen years ago when he left me."

Daphne didn't know what to say. "That won't happen."

"Can you believe, after all these years, he can still affect me like this?"

"I'm sorry."

"I wish he weren't coming."

"Maybe Cam will wake up before he gets here, and he can turn around before he even arrives."

"And yet…"

Daphne waited for the woman to collect herself and finish.

"And yet, I want to see him." She searched Daphne's face. "It's horrible, isn't it? I want to see him badly."

This was so far beyond the scope of Daphne's experience, that she had no clue what to do or say. "Maybe some hot coffee will make you feel better."

Daphne left the infirmary and took the stairs to the third floor for breakfast, the whole time thinking about the mysterious impact of love. If Daphne chose to stay with Brock, would she be like this seventeen years from now, wanting and not wanting to see Cam?

And if—she could barely allow herself to imagine it—if she left Brock for Cam, would it be the same?

Stan was waiting for her alone at a table. "There you are, kiddo. You really do take long showers."

She blushed again. "Sorry. I was talking to Cam's mom."

"No worries. You have about twenty minutes still before the meeting starts."

"Have you eaten?" she asked.

"Yeah. I'd eaten earlier, before getting you the clothes. But I could use another coffee."

He refilled his cup while she went through the buffet with her tray, and then they met up again at the table.

"I'm glad we have a few minutes to chat," Stan said before taking a sip of his coffee.

"Me, too."

"I never had the chance to tell you personally how happy I am that you came back."

She smiled. "Thanks. But I don't know how much help I'll be."

"Don't forget about the cameras."

She nearly had. It was so easy to do sometimes. "I know. But I don't think I make a good Caliban."

"A what?"

She explained to him what she meant.

"Seriously?" He shook his head. "It's not like that at all."

She was beginning to believe him. Maybe if she'd seen the place before it had been corrupted by the subscribers, she could believe him.

"You asked me the other day if I wanted to live a normal life away from here," he said. "And the answer is no. When my wife left me, life became an empty void. This place fills that void like nothing else."

"You get to have fun and help people at the same time."

"Exactly." Then he added, "And you can't beat this location. Am I right, kiddo?"

She nodded.

He leaned in across the table and whispered, "You look pretty cute in my clothes, by the way."

Daphne laughed and punched Stan in the arm. "Oh, hush."

When she and Stan arrived at the planning room, everyone else from the previous evening, except for Cam and Dr. Rose, was already seated, including Emma. Dr. Gray sat on the end, as before, but in Dr. Rose's place was Dr. Reynolds. Daphne imagined him when he was a young teen, embracing Hortense Gray in the back garden of their adoptive father's house. Life could be so strange. Stranger than fiction.

She took her seat and returned everyone's "hellos" and "good mornings."

Dave asked, "Isn't that Stan's shirt?"

Daphne nodded.

"Looks better on her, doesn't it?" Stan laughed.

"The jury's still out on that," Dave replied. "Vince, what do you think? Who's cuter?"

Vince's face turned bright red. He glanced at his father and then shook his head in his usual mute way.

Dave laughed irreverently, uninhibited by the presence of the adults, and said, "Guess it's a tie."

Then Dr. Gray cleared her throat, and everyone went silent.

"As we discussed yesterday, Dr. Rose and I came up with a plan to encourage the subscribers to flee," she said.

"Where is Dr. Rose?" Daphne asked.

"Monitoring the live streams," Stan said.

"One of us doctors must be in the surveillance room at all times," Dr. Gray explained.

"Which is why I missed yesterday's meeting," Lee Reynolds added.

"Oh," Daphne said, a little embarrassed for having interrupted.

"Anyway, this new mission will rely heavily on the acting abilities of you, Daphne," Dr. Gray said. "We hope we can depend on you."

"She can do it," Stan said.

Daphne swallowed hard. She wasn't a very good actress. "I guess it depends on what you want me to do."

"When Cameron awakes, he'll have amnesia," Hortense said.

"How will Cam know to pretend?" Stan asked.

"I told him before he went under," Hortense said, "but we'll take him away for *tests* in the planning room and fill him in on his role, in case he's too groggy to recall when he awakes."

"Got it," Stan said.

"The amnesia will anger you, Daphne," Hortense continued. "It will anger you so much, that you'll leave on the next boat to Ventura, promising to send back the FBI. I'll have Gregory go with you. The subscribers will easily believe that his anger over losing Emma would make him want to help you close our facility down."

"Then what?" Daphne asked.

"You wait. We'll do the rest. I have some contacts I will call in to help—the marksman I've used before, and his team."

"Won't the watchers recognize them?" Greg asked.

"They always wear nylons," Hortense said. "So I doubt it."

"What about Cam's mom?" Daphne asked.

"She can stay or go. It'll be her choice," Hortense replied.

"What if this doesn't work?" Dave asked. "What if the subscribers don't leave?"

"This is our one shot to make it happen," Lee Reynolds said. "They won't ever buy into this scenario again."

"We'll increase the stakes until they go," Hortense said, glancing across the table at Lee.

"What does that mean?" Greg asked.

"It means it's going to get really ugly and really dangerous, but we see no way around it," his mother said.

"I should stay then," Greg argued, putting a protective arm around Emma.

"I want you to take Daphne to our hotel in Ventura," his mother said. "The two of you can watch the live stream from there. I'll let you know when it's safe to come back."

Greg leaned his elbows on the table. "I wish Emma could come with us."

"So do I," Emma said.

Hortense Gray stood up and looked out of the window. "I wish so, too. I really do, but we can't risk it. Believe me, I hate seeing her cooped up. It's one of the reasons this mission is so necessary right now."

"When will this all begin?" Daphne asked.

"We need to hurry up and do this before Carl Turner arrives," Lee Reynolds said. "We don't want him to get any ideas of helping you."

"That would be embarrassing," Stan said. "Imagine the real FBI showing up in the middle of our exercise."

Everyone laughed.

"We'll begin after lunch," Hortense said.

"How long do you think Cam's old man will hang around?" Dave asked.

"Not long," Hortense replied. "Cam will have a miraculous recovery."

CHAPTER SEVENTEEN

Live Performance

After taking a hot cup of coffee down to Mrs. Turner, who refused to leave Cam's side, Daphne returned to her room and took a nap. Sometime later, she was awakened by a knock at her door. It was Bridget with a heap of clothing draped over an arm.

"Hey, girl!" Bridget said. "It's so good to see you again."

"Oh, hi, Bridget. Come on in. What do you have there?"

Bridget came in the room as Daphne closed the door behind her.

"Well, I heard you didn't have any more clean clothes, so I brought you some to borrow."

"Wow. That's so nice."

"We have a laundry room, but I doubted you'd have time to wash clothes." Bridget laid two dresses, a pair of jeans, and three tops out on the bed. She also had four pair of bikini panties. "You can keep the underwear. I have a ton."

"So I guess you heard about Cam," Daphne said.

"I was able to catch some of the live stream over at Marty's—I mean the farmhouse at Christy Ranch. I couldn't always tell what was really going on, especially between the two of you."

Daphne felt the heat rush to her face. "Well, he's in a drug-induced coma right now, which makes me really nervous. But I think they're waking him up today."

"Yeah. It's too dangerous to leave a patient under general anesthesia for more than twenty-four hours. I think Philip's waking him up now."

"What a relief." She wondered about Cam's mom, though.

"Apparently the other doctors wanted to run a few tests. They went off livestream for a while, so they must have taken him to the planning room. I saw you got to visit that yesterday. Pretty cool, huh?"

Daphne shrugged. It really had been cool to see the full behind-the-scenes of this place. "Mind if I change into those jeans?"

"Not at all. That's why I brought them."

Along with the jeans, Daphne grabbed a pair of clean underwear—her real reason for wanting to change—and one of the tops and took them with her to the bathroom. Even though Bridget was taller, the clothes fit perfectly.

"You rock those jeans," Bridget said, when Daphne returned from the bathroom.

"Thanks."

"You have a much better butt than me. You should keep them."

"Seriously?"

"Sure."

"Thanks. They feel comfortable."

"So, you want to grab some lunch?"

Daphne still felt full from breakfast, but she didn't want to disappoint Bridget, and she was also anxious to see Cam, so she slipped on her boots and the two of them made their way to the main building.

"I just want you to know something," Bridget said confidentially. "Cam and I were never really a thing. I mean, I liked him, and he liked me, but it was just a fling. So I don't want you to feel awkward around me, okay?"

"Why would I feel awkward?" Daphne asked, not ready to admit, even to herself, that she and Cam might be more than friends.

"Okay, girlfriend," Bridget said. "Whatever you say."

First, they stopped at the infirmary, but Mrs. Turner said Cam wasn't back from having tests. The poor woman had dark circles under her eyes and was so exhausted that she slurred her speech.

"You should go back to your room and get some rest," Daphne said.

"I can't rest until I see my boy."

"Then come have lunch with us," Daphne suggested.

"My stomach is too upset. I'll eat after I see Cameron."

Daphne and Bridget made small talk with Mrs. Turner for a few more minutes and then went upstairs for lunch.

Vince and Dave were finishing up, but the two girls filled their trays and joined them anyway. They visited with them—mostly Dave since Vince rarely spoke—until they left. Then Bridget told Daphne a little about the exercise she'd been involved in with a new patient named Lisa. During their horseback riding excursion, Bridget and Lisa became separated from the rest of the group and eventually "lost" their horses. They'd been to a cave on Sierra Blanca, to the bunkhouse at Christy Ranch, where they saw the ghost, played by Marty. Then Bridget abandoned Lisa, so that she could get lost on the island.

"The doctors believe that getting lost helps the patients find themselves," Bridget explained as she cut into the chicken breast on her plate. "I think they're right. Don't you?"

Daphne recalled her time "lost" on the island. She'd first tried to drown herself in the stream in Central Valley but then had decided to fight for her life. Climbing the bluffs, enduring the heat and sunburn, going without food and water, and running from danger had made her feel more connected to the earth and to herself.

"Daphne?" Bridget asked, stirring Daphne from her reverie. "You okay?"

"Yeah. Just thinking."

"About?"

"How strange life can be."

"Especially here. Am I right?"

Daphne smiled, but, as she recalled Malcolm Gray and his orphan subjects, she added, "Everywhere, really."

Stan came up to them at that moment. "Cam's awake and back at his room in the infirmary."

Daphne stood up.

"Brace yourself," he said.

"What's wrong?" Bridget asked.

Daphne didn't wait to hear what Stan had to say. Since she couldn't believe a word he said in front of the cameras, she had to go and see Cam for herself. Worried that a drug-induced coma could have real side-effects, she raced from the room and climbed down the stairs to the second floor. Then she ran down the hall and bolted into the infirmary.

Both Cam and his mother looked up at her as she entered the room.

"Cam?" Daphne stopped just inside the door.

He looked at his mom, who patted his hands as tears streamed down her cheeks.

"Daphne is your next-door neighbor," Mrs. Turner said. "She's been your friend for many, many years, sweet boy."

"What?" Bridget said as she brushed by Daphne, panting. "Cam, don't you know who she is?"

Either Bridget was an excellent actress, or she didn't know what was going on.

Maybe they didn't have enough faith in Daphne's acting skills, so they had Bridget tag along to help. That would explain why she had run to catch up with Daphne.

"The doctor says to give him time," Mrs. Turner said. "He says it's common for people who've been in a coma to need time coming out of it."

"So this is temporary?" Daphne asked, moving to Cam's side. She avoided direct eye contact with him, worried she'd bust out with inappropriate laughter. Who knew what her nerves would make her do?

"Dr. Johnson seems confident that it is," Mrs. Turner said. "I'm just so relieved you're awake, sweet boy. I've been worried sick."

"Something clicked in my head when you said 'sweet boy,'" Cam said to his mother. "Haven't you always called me that?"

"Since you were a baby," his mom said.

"I think I somehow knew that. And I recognize your face."

Mrs. Turner leaned over and kissed him on his forehead. Daphne was glad that Cam was trying to make this as easy as possible on his mother.

"But you don't recognize me?" Daphne asked.

"Or me?" Bridget added.

He looked from one to the other and shook his head. "No. Sorry."

Bridget broke out in tears. "We've been friends for over a year."

"Just give him time, dear," Mrs. Turner said again.

"Now that he's awake, maybe you should try to get some food in your system," Daphne suggested. She needed to get rid of Cam's mom. She didn't want to explode in front of her and upset her any more than necessary.

"Oh, I suppose I should. I just hate to leave him now that I can finally talk to him."

"I'm not going anywhere, Ma."

His mother smiled. "You sound just like your old self."

She kissed him once more and left the room. Daphne opened the door to the reception area and waited for Mrs. Turner to disappear, and then she turned to the girl behind the desk. "I want to see one of the doctors right now. Please get one of them over here. I don't care which one, but I'm upset, and I need to see one of them *now*."

Daphne returned to Cam's room and paced the floor.

"Daphne?" Bridget asked.

It was time to perform her very best act. She knew the subscribers were watching, and she knew the Calibans were depending on her.

"Listen to me," Daphne began. "I know you love it here, but the doctors take too many serious risks with people's lives. I can't take this anymore. Not when it has hurt my best friend. He doesn't even recognize us."

Real tears actually stung Daphne's eyes as she looked over at Cam's blank face. He was doing an amazing job with his part of the show. He really did seem confused.

"Daphne, calm down," Bridget said. "His amnesia's temporary."

Hortense Gray entered the room. "You wanted to see me, Daphne?"

Daphne took a deep breath, and, as she let it out, she recalled everything she had felt in the past about the Purgatorium. She recalled her original mission to save Cam, before she knew Emma was alive and the subscribers were the bad guys.

"Did you know that Cam can't even remember who I am?" Daphne demanded. "He's been my best friend since I was a little girl, no more than three years old. He's been my brother's only friend through all of his problems. Cam is the one who taught us how to play street kickball and how to ding-dong-ditch. We turned his treehouse into our personal clubhouse and hangout. He showed my sister, Kara, how to moonwalk when she had an eighties dance at school." The tears were streaming from Daphne's eyes, like the whole thing was real. Her hands trembled, and her knees weakened, and her nose was so stuffed she could barely breathe. "He started a band and invited us to join, even though we weren't as musical as he was. He's been a rock in my life, a light at the end of a dark tunnel, a beacon of hope in a world that can sometimes be so cruel. I love him with all my heart and now he may be lost to me forever. He may never remember who I am!"

"You need to calm down," Dr. Gray said.

"No! You need to listen to me for once." Daphne flailed her arms dramatically. "I can appreciate that you want to save people. That's great. You even had me going for a while—inviting me to the planning room and everything. But what's happened to Cam has reminded me why I came back here in the first place. You go too far. Look at what happened to Emma!"

"That was an accident," Dr. Gray said.

"Sure. You go ahead and lie to yourself, because you're the only one who believes it."

Dr. Gray harrumphed.

"And this thing with Cam?" Daphne continued. "This was irresponsible medicine. You may have just robbed me of the best part of my life since Kara's death. Well, you're messing with the wrong girl! I'm not going to let you do this to another single person."

She was on a roll—on a high—and almost added that she had dragon flames!

Dr. Gray crossed her arms. "What are you saying?"

"I'm saying that I'm going to get on the first boat out of here, and I'm going to let the police know what's going on down here."

"The police have already been here, and they did nothing."

Daphne lifted her arms in the air. "I mean the FBI!"

"And why should they listen to you? It's not like you have any evidence of any wrongdoing."

"Oh, yes I do." Daphne walked around Cam's bed and stood right in front of Dr. Gray. "Not only did I record a private conversation I had with Dr. Rose and Dr. Lee, but I also have your father's journal!"

Hortense's mouth dropped open. "You what?"

Daphne covered her mouth with her hand. She hadn't meant to say that. Now Greg was probably in big trouble.

"Where did you get that?" Hortense Gray asked, her bottom lip trembling slightly.

"I stole it from your office."

"I don't keep it in my office."

"It doesn't matter. I have it, and I have some of my own surveillance, and I'm going to show it all to the FBI as soon as possible. So if I were you, I'd be very afraid. You're facing criminal charges for this!"

Daphne turned to Cam, whose face looked as shocked as Dr. Gray's. "I know you're confused right now, but I'll be back. I promise you."

In the spirit of her performance, which didn't feel at all like a performance, she leaned over and planted a kiss on Cam's mouth. Then she left the room.

Dr. Gray followed after her. "I'll make you a deal!"

Daphne turned. "There's nothing you can say to stop me."

"At least let me have a private word with you."

Dr. Gray wanted to talk to Daphne in the planning room, but Daphne didn't want to be confronted about the journal.

"Like I said, there's nothing you can say."

Daphne turned on her heel and stormed down the hallway. Greg emerged from the other end and said, "Let me come with you."

"Why should I trust you?" Daphne kept walking.

"Because I've been looking for a way to shut this place down ever since Emma's death."

"Then come on." She brushed past him.

Greg kept his feet planted and faced his mother, who still stood in the hallway, shocked. "And I'm the one who gave her Malcolm's journal."

Then he and Daphne turned the corner and ran.

CHAPTER EIGHTEEN

Ventura

It took most of the day for Daphne and Greg to travel from the resort to the hotel in Ventura. First, they had packed and loaded their gear on a jeep. Greg had refused Roger's offer to drive them to Prisoners Harbor. He had insisted that Roger and Stan follow them in another jeep so Greg could drive them himself. Both Roger and Stan had tried to talk them out of leaving—although Stan had been acting. Stan had been such a good actor, that at one point, Daphne had begun to believe the plan had changed.

Greg had said if they wanted the jeep back, they'd have to follow. He already had the keys.

Once she and Greg had finally got to Prisoners Harbor, they had waited at the pier in the heat among the squawking pelicans and sea gulls for two hours for a boat that could take them. The boat ride itself was another hour, though it was made better by a humpback sighting. The cab ride from the port at Ventura was another half hour. By the time they had carried their things up the elevator to their fifth-floor suite, Daphne was starving.

"Let's order room service, so we can get on the live stream right away," Greg suggested.

He took his laptop from his bag, plugged it into the wall with a charger, and connected to the internet. Then he grabbed an HDMI cord and fed it into the big, flat screen TV in their suite. In a few more minutes, he had several windows open on the television, each showing a different scene.

Daphne asked, "If the island doesn't have internet…"

"Oh, it has internet," Greg said. "That's how we send the feed out to our subscribers."

"But your mom said…"

"She tells everyone that."

"What about cell phone service?" she asked.

"There's one hot spot," Greg said. "My mom has Roger take her up to a hill by the naval tower once a week so she can return her calls."

As Greg finished setting up the stream, he said, "Your performance was magnificent, by the way. I always knew you had it in you."

"I was terrified."

"But it was fun, too, right?" He looked up at her, and she nodded. "Not everyone was sure if you could pull it off."

"That's why they sent Bridget, isn't it?" she asked.

"It was that obvious, huh?"

"She's such a natural." Then she said, "I hope I didn't get you in trouble, mentioning the journal."

Greg blushed. "What's done is done. Do you still have it?"

Daphne took it from her backpack and handed it over. "It's so…" she was going to say heartbreaking, but Greg interrupted with, "I know."

When he said nothing more about it, she asked, "What do you want to eat?"

Daphne got to work calling in their food order, and then she turned her attention to the television. One of the windows showed Cam's room in the infirmary. He sat up in the bed with his mother beside him. Daphne couldn't hear what they were saying, but they both seemed happy. His mother had showered and changed and had even put on makeup. The dress she wore was also flattering, and Daphne suspected it had all been done for Carl Turner, due to arrive any minute.

On another screen, Toni was being embraced by her mother in one of the cabana units. They were both crying and sitting on the edge of the bed, rocking back and forth.

"What's going on there?" Daphne asked.

Greg clicked a key on his laptop, and the window with Toni enlarged. The other windows were still visible in a row across the bottom of the screen, but the one in the center was large, and now Daphne could hear what Toni and her mother were saying.

"I don't know, darling," the mother said. "I just don't know."

"I'm his own flesh and blood." Toni pulled her scarf further down on her head, a gesture that reminded Daphne of her Limuw ceremony and its aftermath.

"He knows that. It's just hard on him. He's losing a son."

"You've said that a million times to me," Toni stood up and faced her mother, who remained seated on the bed. "I'm sick of hearing that. When are you going to understand that you never had a son? I've always been a daughter. From the very beginning, it was always me. I haven't changed at all. Not a bit. No one has died."

"I guess it's your father's idea of you then. He's mourning his idea of you, baby."

"His fantasy. What he hoped I would be, but not what I am and always have been. Why can't he love me for just me?"

"He will. Give him time."

Daphne and Greg exchanged glances.

"Poor Toni," Daphne said.

Just then, Toni's father entered the unit in his bathing suit, with a towel draped over his shoulder. Toni left the room and went to the bathroom.

"Have a good swim, baby?" Toni's mother asked.

"Somewhat." He crossed to his bag and dug out clean clothes. "That pool is something else, ain't it? Especially at night, when it's all lit up."

Daphne hadn't had the chance to swim in it during this last trip. She had meant to take another look at the amazing underwater aquarium.

"Sure is, but aren't you freezing?"

"Nah."

Instead of waiting for the restroom, he changed right there in the room.

Daphne covered her eyes. "Oh, gross."

Greg laughed. "It happens."

Thankfully, their room service arrived, and Daphne could finally eat. She and Greg made themselves comfortable on the sofa, she with her burger and fries and he with his steak and potatoes, using the coffee table for their trays.

Toni had come from the restroom, but she hadn't acknowledged her father.

"I guess I'll go back to my own room," Toni said.

When she opened the door, a masked man bent her arm behind her back and put a gun to her head in the doorway. Toni's mother screamed as the gunman moved inside and kicked the door closed behind him.

At first, Daphne couldn't tell who it was, because the gunman wore baggy clothes and a ski mask, but when he spoke, she recognized Dave's voice.

"Empty your wallet and give me your watch, or she dies."

Toni's parents stared back in shock, neither moving.

"Oh my God," the mother said.

Dave shot the bulb in the bedside lamp. Both parents ducked, and the mother screamed again.

Daphne wondered if Dave enjoyed shooting a real bullet into the room. Was he thrilled? Terrified?

"Make it fast," Dave ordered, as he pressed the barrel of the gun against Toni's temple.

Toni's eyes were stretched wide open. Daphne didn't think Toni realized this was just an exercise. She looked too frightened. But maybe she was a good actress.

"Okay, calm down," Toni's father said, as he fumbled for his wallet, which was in a pair of jeans on the floor.

"Don't hurt my baby," Toni's mom begged. "We'll give you what you want."

Toni's father threw a wad of bills on the floor at Dave's feet.

"Pick them up and put them in my pocket," Dave said.

His hands shaking like an epileptic, Toni's dad obeyed.

Dave shoved Toni into her father and ran.

Toni's dad embraced her. "You okay?"

She nodded with her face in his chest.

Her father tightened his hold on her as Toni's mother embraced them from behind.

Daphne suddenly realized she was crying.

"I'm sorry," Toni said, coming up for air.

"It's just money," her father said.

"No. I mean I'm sorry that who I am is hurtful to you."

Toni's dad's mouth dropped open. He wiped his eyes and shook his head. Then he put his arms around Toni once more and wept.

Daphne wiped her eyes and noticed Greg doing the same thing.

Then she asked him, "Are you and your mom good now? Or do you still want to leave the island?"

"My mom and I will never be a hundred percent good."

She wasn't sure what to say to that.

"It's been hard only seeing her in the summers," he said.

"I didn't realize…"

"I've gone to boarding school since I was eight years old."

"Oh."

"And even in the summers, she worked the whole time on the island. I kind of had no choice but to get involved if I ever wanted to see her."

"You didn't like going?"

"I loved it. I looked forward to it every year. But when Emma and I started getting serious, we wanted to leave. We wanted a normal life for a while."

"I get that."

"And then I was convinced my mom had caused Emma's death. Then, I thought, 'I'm just a pawn. I don't matter to her at all.' And I wanted out. When I came to you last winter, I was totally, one hundred percent serious, and I was scared. I didn't know what to do."

"Man…"

"And then my world was rocked again when I found out the truth about Emma."

"It must be hard for her, in hiding all these months."

"Are you kidding? She's got it easy. She gets her meals brought in three times a day. She either reads or watches the live stream all day. And once I got back—well, let's just say no one cared how much time I spent with her."

"So you've been having some fun together, huh?"

He blushed.

"What about your dad?"

Greg frowned. "All Arturo Gomez cares about is Arturo Gomez."

"Oh."

"And the island foxes. He cares about those, too," Greg said. "But he doesn't care about me or my mom or anything else except living an exciting life on the island. Drama. That's what he thrives on."

Daphne had been keeping an eye on the window with Cam and his mom, so she noticed someone new entered the room.

"Oh, can we click over to that screen now?" she asked.

Greg took another bite of his steak and then punched a key on his laptop to change the window. Daphne held her breath when the voices became audible.

"Pamela." The man nodded. "You're looking good. I see our boy is finally awake."

So that was Cam's biological father, Daphne realized.

"*Our* boy?" Cam asked.

Carl frowned. "I've come a long way to see you. Are we really going to start out like that?"

"Carl, calm down. Cameron has amnesia." Mrs. Turner squeezed Cam's arm. "This is your biological father. He…"

"You don't recognize me?" Carl asked.

"Sorry," Cam said.

"But you recognize her?" Carl pointed to Pamela.

"I think so," Cam said. "But I've been talking to her all day, and you just arrived. Maybe I'll begin to recognize you, too." Then he added. "Thanks for coming. I hope it wasn't a lot of trouble."

"It was a lot of trouble, son, but the doctor wasn't sure you'd pull through," Carl said, remaining by the door. "I was scared out of my mind the whole way here."

"Well, you can turn back around and go home whenever you'd like," Pamela said. "As you can see, he's awake now."

"That's nice of you, to want to get rid of me so soon, but I'm not going anywhere yet."

Pamela blushed. "Suit yourself."

"As long as you're both here," Cam said, "tell me how you met. I take it you two aren't married anymore?"

No one said anything for a few long moments. Then Carl cleared his throat.

"We knew each other from school," Carl said. "Your mom had a crush on me all through high school."

"Don't flatter yourself," Pamela said.

Carl laughed. "You even said. Don't act like you didn't."

"When did you start seeing each other?" Cam asked.

"We ran into each other after college, at the party of a mutual friend," Pamela said.

"She still had the hots for me," Carl said. "I could see it in her eyes."

Pamela turned red. "Whatever."

"We married not long after that," Carl said. "And you came a few months later."

Pamela crossed her arms and whispered, "Be careful what you say. There are cameras in all the rooms."

"So why did you leave?" Cam asked Carl.

Carl cleared his throat. "When you were born, you became the apple of your mother's eye. I didn't even exist anymore."

"That's not true," Pamela scolded.

"The hell it ain't."

"Don't try to blame this on me."

"I'm not blaming you," Carl said. "The fact of the matter is, I should have been a better man, and I wasn't."

The room grew quiet. Daphne and Greg exchanged glances. The screen showed the all-too clear tears forming in both Cam and his mother's eyes.

After a few moments, Cam asked, "Did I see you much after your divorce?"

Carl lowered his head, as though he were studying the patterns in the floor tile.

"Not for a long time," Pamela said. "I was so angry. I didn't want him around us."

"I had an affair," Carl said. "Your mother was hurt."

"To the core," Pamela said. "I was hurt to the core."

"I'm sorry," Carl said. "I know I can never say that enough."

"How long before I saw you again?" Cam asked, his lips trembling.

"I missed the next twelve years of your life," Carl said. "Until your accident."

Carl was referring to a three-wheeler accident. Daphne was there when it had happened and remembered it vividly. She and Joey had both been there, along with a few other kids, watching Cam try out the new three-wheeler. They'd all taken turns trying it. Cam had gone a little wild and had gone off the edge of a cliff by accident. He broke several ribs and his arm and had punctured a lung. It had been one of the scariest times in Daphne's life. There was a two-day period when Cam was unconscious, and the doctors weren't sure if he'd make it.

"I tried to see you during that first year of your life, and then after that, I was too ashamed," Carl said. "Then my job moved me to D.C. I figured you'd give up on me, and probably resent me, and there wasn't a thing on earth I could do about it. So I just gave up."

"And started over with a new family," Pamela added.

"Basically. That's true. But I never stopped loving either one of you."

Cam covered his face with his hands. His mother sat back down in the chair beside him and clutched the bed rail with a quivering hand.

"I guess I figured you'd call or write to me if you ever wanted to see me," Carl added.

Daphne turned to Greg. "Why do estranged parents put the burden of building the relationship on their children? That's the same kind of thing that's happened to Vince. Cam said Lee makes no effort, and so Vince just goes with the flow, miserable."

"That's true," Greg said. "I guess even parents are afraid."

"Carl should have known better." Daphne was livid. It killed her that she was in Ventura instead of in the room with Cam, where she could comfort him.

"Why haven't you ever told him this before?" Pamela asked, drawing Daphne's attention back to the screen.

Carl shrugged. "This is the first time he's asked without getting all accusatory. I guess his amnesia has made him a better listener to what I have to say. I tried, Pamela. That time he was in that accident, and we were in the hospital just like this, he told me to get out. He wanted Fred by his side."

Carl moved closer to the bed and put a hand on Cam's shoulder. "I'm sorry it's such a sad story, son. You can't remember this now, but you've spent most of your life preferring your stepdad to me. His name's Fred. He's actually a decent human being. I'm glad you had him watching out for you."

Daphne wondered what was going on inside Cam's head, since he was only pretending not to know his father and their past. Was he holding back accusatory thoughts? Did he have corrections he wanted to make to Carl's story? Or did he want to tell his side of what he remembered from his childhood?

"I wish I was there," Daphne said, feeling stuffed from her dinner. She got up and stretched her gut. "I wish I could be there to help Cam."

At that moment the hotel telephone rang. Daphne and Greg glanced at one another in surprise.

Greg got up and answered the phone on the desk across the room. "Hello? Yes, sir." He held out the receiver toward Daphne. "It's for you."

<u>CHAPTER NINETEEN</u>

The Best Laid Plans

Daphne's eyebrows shot up. Who would be calling her here?

She took the phone from Greg. "Hello?"

"God, Daphne. Are you trying to give your mother and me a heart attack?"

"Dad?"

"Tell me you're okay."

"I'm fine. How did you get this number?"

"Dr. Gray finally returned my messages. She told me this is where I should reach you."

"You spoke to her on the phone?"

"Listen to me, Daphne. Are you listening?"

"Yes. I'm listening."

"First thing I want you to do is charge your phone. I've been trying to reach you for two days."

She pulled her phone from her pocket, not having realized she'd let it die. "Okay. I'll plug it in as soon as we hang up."

"I've texted you a boarding pass. Use it to fly home tomorrow. Your flight leaves at noon. Southwest Airlines. Got that?"

"But, Dad, my spring break doesn't end for a few more…"

"Don't 'but Dad' me, Daphne. You do as I say. Is that clear? Your mom and I have been put through the ringer these past couple of days. How could you lie to us like that?"

"Mrs. Turner needed my help and…"

"And that woman will get an earful when she returns. I promise you that."

"Dad, I'm sorry."

"Charge your phone. Check your messages for that boarding pass. And be sure to call Brock. He's as worried as we are."

"Okay."

"I'll see you at the airport tomorrow afternoon. I'll pick you up in front of the baggage claim."

Daphne's stomach clenched. "Okay."

She hung up the hotel phone and said, "Dang."

"You okay?"

"My parents are making me fly home tomorrow." She rummaged through her bag for one of the portable phone chargers.

"I'll text you the link to the live stream along with the passcode, so you can keep up."

That made her feel better, though the thought of not seeing Cam again in person before she left—she stopped herself from finishing that thought. She needed to call Brock.

She plugged in her phone to charge as she looked at what Greg was pointing at on the screen.

"That's Lisa. The new girl."

It was nighttime and a far-away shot, so the figure scaling the bluff on the side opposite the boardwalk wasn't easy to make out until she appeared in another window at a closer angle on the summit, gasping for air. Daphne had made that same climb just before Brock had shown up to witness her dive into the sea.

Greg switched that window to the center position on the screen, so Daphne could see the newcomer in better detail.

Lisa looked to be Indian—not Native American Indian, but Far East Indian, and a little older than Daphne—maybe nineteen or twenty. Her straight black hair, which she kept pushing behind her ears, was shoulder length. Her dark eyes were round and red-rimmed. She continually chewed the inside of her full lips as she gazed out across the crashing waves, audible now through the hotel television.

Greg stood up. "There goes Stan."

Greg pointed at another screen on the bottom of the television, showing Stan running past the main building toward the boardwalk, taking the steps two at a time.

"He thinks she's going to jump," Greg added.

"No one stopped *me*," Daphne said.

"It's a lot more dangerous at night. And when *you* jumped, the tide was receding. Right now, the waves are crazy violent."

"Oh."

Lisa backed up several steps, like she was going to make a run for it before leaping into the ocean. Stan reached the top of the board walk and ran toward the bluff.

Lisa charged across the summit toward the sea. Daphne's heart raced.

"No!" Daphne said out loud at the same time Stan did on the screen.

"Lisa, no!" Stan's voice carried onto Lisa's screen.

Lisa stopped, tottering on the edge. For a moment, Daphne closed her eyes, unable to watch. When she opened them, Stan had Lisa in his arms, and she was sobbing violently into his shoulder.

"That was close," Greg said.

Then something unexpected happened on the screen. Lisa lifted her tear-stained face and cupped Stan's cheeks.

"Thank you," she said, just before she kissed him.

And it wasn't a peck.

Lisa laid it on thick!

"Oh my gosh!" Daphne said, smiling.

Stan wrapped his arms more tightly around Lisa's waist and kissed her hard.

"Go, Stan!" Greg shouted.

Daphne and Greg busted out in laughter. Greg offered Daphne a fist, and she bumped it with her own.

Then her phone pinged—again and again and again, reminding her that she had messages. Before checking them, she took her phone to the bedroom to call Brock.

"I'll be right back," she said to Greg before closing her door.

She dialed Brock's number.

"Daphne?" Brock's voice came through the phone.

She trembled a little, and her knees went weak, so she sat on the bed and cleared her dry throat. "Hi, Brock."

She felt so bad, so guilty, and so weird, like she was disconnected from him and from herself.

"Are you okay?" he asked. "Where are you?"

"I'm fine. I'm at a hotel in Ventura. I fly in tomorrow."

"Good."

"So, I guess I'll see you sometime tomorrow then," she said.

"Hold on. What happened at the resort? Were you able to talk some sense into the Calibans?"

"It's a long story. I'll tell you about it tomorrow. I'm tired."

"Okay. It's good to hear your voice."

She swallowed the lump in her throat. "It's good to hear yours, too."

"Have a safe flight."

"Thanks."

"I love you."

"I love you, too." She hung up and then fell, face first, onto the bed and cried.

After a few minutes, her phone pinged again. She dried her eyes and decided it was time to read her messages.

She scrolled down to the earliest one, so she could read them in order.

Saturday: March 16: 2:31 p.m.: Brock: I miss you already. Hope you have a great time in Galveston.

Saturday: March 16: 10:07 p.m.: Brock: Watching Big Bang Theory and thinking of you.

Sunday: March 17: 12:07 p.m.: Brock: Having fun? Text me back so I know you're alive.

Sunday: March 17: 8:47 p.m.: Brock: Daphne this isn't nice. Answer me.

Monday: March 18: 9:20 a.m.: Brock: If you don't call me right now, I'm driving to Galveston to look for you.

Monday: March 18: 9:53 a.m.: Mom: Call me asap.

Monday: March 18: 10:55 a.m.: Dad: We've filed a missing person's report and are worried sick. Call as soon as you can.

Monday: March 18: 11:50 a.m.: Brock: Your parents are pissed. So am I. Where are you? I know you aren't with Mandy. What's going on?

Monday: March 18: 4:38 p.m.: Brock: Just got a call from Arturo Gomez. No frickin way. Why?

Monday: March 18: 5:15 p.m.: Dad: Can't believe you would do this to us after all we've been through. Brock is on his way to bring you home.

Tuesday: March 19: 11:15 a.m.: Mom: I feel so helpless while I wait to hear if you're okay. I can't wait to see your face.

Tuesday: March 19: 6:42 p.m.: Brock: Still in Ventura. Hate the way we left things. Tried to get a ride back to the island, but there's nothing until morning.

Wednesday: March 20: 10:15 a.m.: Brock: Decided just to fly home. Doubt anything I say would change your mind. Come home as soon as you can. I love you.

Wednesday: March 20: 5:11 p.m.: Unknown: This is Giovanni. Good news. My foster parents picked me up. Yeah, they brought me back to Sacramento. They listened to all I had to say and went back to the Feds. Same ones they talked to when they left last summer. Yeah, not FBI. It's something like ATF—The Federal Bureau of Alcohol, Tobacco, and Firearms. My parents told them about the real bullets. This time they're listening. So, yeah. Good news.

Wednesday: March 20: 6:20 a.m.: Unknown: You won't believe it. Yeah, the feds tapped into the island's surveillance. They asked me to point out things and people. I saw you!

Wednesday: March 20: 7:36 p.m.: Unknown: Yeah, so they're making me go back to the island, to show the ATF officers or whatever where to go. Maybe I'll see you soon. Hope so. Your friend, Giovanni

"Oh my God!" Daphne jumped from the bed and rushed out to the sitting room, where Greg looked up from the sofa.

"What's wrong?" he asked.

"Giovanni and his parents," Daphne spit out, almost tongue-tied. "They're going back to the island with some federal officers to investigate."

"Giovanni?" Greg took out his phone and punched at his screen.

"Who are you calling?"

"I'm leaving a message for my mom. Hold on. Mom, this is Gregory. Giovanni texted Daphne about returning there with federal agents. Is this part of your plan? I didn't think you and Giovanni were in touch. Call or text when you can or signal me through the live stream. Bye."

"So, you think it's possible that Giovanni is part of your mom's plan?"

"It's possible, but then why would he be texting you about it? That's the part that doesn't make sense."

She sat next to him on the sofa and took a sip of her iced tea. "Well, Giovanni says they hacked into the surveillance."

"Oh, no," Greg said. He stood up and paced around. "Oh, no. That's the worst thing that could happen. They won't understand that everyone is acting. Oh, crap. Oh, hell."

He took out his phone and punched the screen again. "Mom, it's me again. The surveillance has been hacked by feds. Call me."

He hung up and continued his pacing.

"Now what?" Daphne asked. "What do you think is gonna happen?"

"They'll arrest everyone, that's what. Holy crap."

CHAPTER TWENTY

Stuck in San Antonio

During her layover in Dallas the next day, Daphne opened the link Greg had texted for the live stream and entered the passcode. It was hard to see details on her phone, but she was able to make out Cam's mom and dad leaving with their luggage on a jeep with Roger toward Prisoners Harbor. Before falling asleep the night before, she'd witnessed Cam make a full "recovery," to the great relief of his parents.

She really wished Cam had decided to leave the island with them.

She'd tried to call and text Giovanni, but her call went straight to voicemail, and her texts remained unanswered; yet there'd been no sign of him or any federal agents on the live stream.

When her parents picked her up at the airport, they were red-hot angry at her. They refused to speak. Joey wouldn't even look at her when she said hello. She sat beside him in the backseat of the Honda Pilot and sobbed.

They didn't understand.

When they pulled into their driveway, Brock's Charger was parked out front, and he was leaning against it with his arms crossed. Daphne's heart fluttered. She wanted and didn't want to see him all at the same time.

Unlike her family, Brock opened her door and smiled as soon as he saw her, sweeping her up in a tight embrace. Her father popped the hatch to the back and asked Brock if he could help with her backpack.

Once they were inside the house, Daphne found her laptop and hooked it up to the television in the family room, just as Greg had done back at their hotel.

"I want you to see," she said to them all. "I want you to understand why I went back to the island to save Cam. I want you to see what's going on."

Her family and Brock gathered around the television—reluctantly, it seemed to her. They were all hurt and mad, and the last thing they wanted to do was listen to her try to explain.

"I know y'all love Dr. Gray," she said to her parents from where she sat on the sofa beside Brock. "But you have to admit, things got out of hand last summer. Mrs. Turner tried to get you to help, but you've been too swept up by Joey's progress."

"Watch your tone," her father said from his recliner.

"And choose your words more carefully," her mother warned.

Daphne went on to explain what Dr. Gray had told her—how her original vision of living art as therapy got messed up by the subscribers, because they wanted riskier entertainment. She told them the plan to trick the subscribers into fleeing and about Giovanni's texts.

"Why don't the doctors just take away their services?" her mom asked. "Why this elaborate scheme?"

"Yeah," her father agreed. "Just cut them off."

Daphne explained about the threats of blackmail.

"They can't be serious about that," her dad said. "They'd only incriminate themselves. Dr. Gray should see that."

"Are you sure she wasn't just trying to get you off the island?" Brock asked.

None of them understood. "Never mind." She got up and unplugged her laptop from the television. "I'm sorry I was so much trouble." She fought back the tears gathering behind her lids.

She headed down the hall for her room, planning to leave them all, even Brock, behind, when her mother said, "Wait, Daphne."

Her mother put her hands on Daphne's shoulders and said, "I know you wanted to help. I'm sorry it didn't work out. But please don't ever make us worry like that again. Okay?"

Daphne nodded, unable to speak, because of the lump in her throat and the tears that were threatening to pour.

Her mother hugged her, with the laptop between them, and then hastened to the kitchen, batting away tears.

Daphne glanced back at her father, who avoided her eyes. She supposed he needed more time. Joey went to his room without a word. Brock followed Daphne to hers.

"You want to go get some tacos or something?" he asked.

"I'm not hungry."

"We could go for a drive."

"I'm tired." She put her laptop on her desk but held back the urge to watch what was going on at the resort. She didn't want to be rude. Her attitude was hurtful enough.

"I'm sorry I didn't stay there with you," he finally said.

Tears poured from her eyes—she couldn't hold them back anymore. "I really thought you'd stay."

"I really thought you'd follow me. I thought for sure you'd get on the next boat out, once you saw I was serious. I even waited in Ventura, hoping."

"I'm sorry."

He brushed away her tears with his shaky fingers. "Come here." Then he planted a soft kiss on her lips.

Daphne felt numb. Too many emotions, especially anxiety over what was happening at the resort, were playing havoc on her mood and her stability. She oscillated between wanting to scream, wanting to cry, and wanting to run away. The most important thing on her mind was watching the live stream, but no one else was interested.

She kissed Brock back and said, "I'm really tired. Why don't we get together this weekend?"

"I've got that meet on Saturday," he reminded her. "Can you make it?"

She gave him a smile. "Of course. I'll be cheering for you."

"What about tomorrow?" he asked her. "My shift at the Y ends at eight-thirty."

"Call me when you get off," she said. "We'll figure something out."

He kissed her again and then said, "I'm so glad you're home."

After he left, she broke down in more tears. Didn't she want to be with him? What was wrong with her?

She took her laptop to bed to watch the live stream alone in her room, when there was a knock at her door.

"Come in," she said.

It was Joey. "Can I watch the feed with you?"

"Really?" She was thrilled. "Sure, come on." She patted the bed beside her.

They sat side-by-side with pillows propped between them and the headboard and the laptop resting partly on her lap and partly on his. She kept clicking through the windows on the screen.

Although she didn't recognize everyone in every window, she saw Vince and Dave playing billiards, Stan and Lisa strolling hand in hand on the beach, and Bridget painting Toni's fingernails in Toni's unit, while Toni's parents slept in their own. She saw all three doctors together in the surveillance room, but they were watching, not speaking. Her heart nearly broke in two when she saw Cam sitting on the edge of the bluff beneath a crescent moon throwing stones into the sea.

"You don't want to watch the doctors?" Joey asked when she kept changing the window at the center of the laptop.

"I'm looking for some sign of the feds," she said to him.

Joey laughed. "Okay, now you sound like me."

She laughed, too. It was true. She did.

The next morning, she woke up to the laptop on the empty side of the bed, where Joey had been the night before, and to her phone ringing. The last thing she remembered was watching the live stream with Joey. She wasn't sure at what point she had conked out. As she picked up her phone to answer it, she saw it was nine in the morning, and Mrs. Turner was calling.

"Hello?"

"Daphne, it's Pamela. Could you come over some time this morning? I have something for you."

"What is it?"

"A letter from Cameron."

"I'll be right over."

Without changing clothes, or putting on deodorant, or so much as brushing her teeth, she slipped on a pair of flip-flops and headed out the door. Her dad was already at work, and her mom was gone, too. Maybe running errands. Joey was probably in his room, either sleeping or playing a video game, or maybe he'd gone with her mom.

She crossed the lawn, forgetting how hot it could be in San Antonio, even in the morning in March. She missed the breeze off the water and the smell of ocean air.

She missed Cam.

As she knocked on Mrs. Turner's door, she worried she should have checked in on Joey and told him where she was going—but she would only be gone a few minutes.

Cam's mom looked radiant when she opened the door. Her eyes were not only rested but beaming with happiness.

"Come in," she said.

Daphne stepped inside the foyer. "I can't stay. Joey's home alone. How's Cam?"

"He was doing just fine when I left him," she said. "And he's promised to visit for a full two weeks in the summer."

Summertime seemed so far away.

Mrs. Turner took an envelope from the granite bar and handed it to Daphne. "Here you go."

It was a plain white envelope with her name on it in Cam's clumsy print. She couldn't wait to rip it open. "Thanks. Maybe I can come back later, once my mom gets home? I'd love to know more about how Cam is doing."

"That would be wonderful, dear. I'll be home all day. Come whenever."

Daphne thanked her again and ran home to read the letter. First, she checked in Joey's room, where he sat at his desk in front of his P.C.

"What are you doing?" she asked.

"I've been watching the live stream."

"How did you get the passcode?"

"I saw you type it in yesterday, and I got the link from your browser."

"Have you been up all night?" He was still wearing the same clothes from yesterday, just like she was, and his brown hair was messy and in his eyes. He blinked against the sunlight slanting through the front window.

"Not *all* night. I slept a few hours. You should watch with me in here. I've got better graphics."

"Wow, you really do. Is this the computer you built yourself?"

He smiled. "Yes. It's better than anything you can buy already assembled."

She leaned against the door frame and crossed her arms. "You learned how to do this at school?"

"Are you kidding? I'm just taking basic courses right now. I could teach the college algebra class I'm in. Too bad my professor doesn't know I read calculus theory for fun."

"You should tell him."

"I'm not sure that would go over well."

"You could be right."

"In fact, I just learned a new math proof—not from school, but from a website—showing how one can equal zero. My friend, Judge William Clark—" He stopped himself, probably because he knew there really was no Judge William Clark. Old habits were hard to break.

Daphne had been told not to walk on eggshells around him. "One can't equal zero."

"Sure, it can. Want to see?"

She uncrossed her arms and stuffed her hands in her pockets. "I thought math was supposed to be an exact science."

"Science isn't even an exact science."

Her phone pinged. She was reluctant to answer, because she expected it to be Brock with a sweet message to make her feel guilty, but it was Greg.

Are you seeing this?

To Joey, she said, "Well, show me the proof later. Tell me what's happening on the island."

"I think the feds arrived this morning or maybe late last night."

Daphne sat on the edge of the bed behind Joey's desk chair and peered at the scene over his shoulder. "What makes you think that?"

He unmuted his screen. "Listen."

Hortense Gray and Arturo Gomez stood on the sidewalk at the top of the canyon ridge where the jeeps were always parked. They stood facing two men. One held the leash of a black dog sitting obediently between them and the other held a piece of paper in his hands. They wore matching green uniforms with a gold insignia on the left breast pocket and on the front of their caps. They were also armed with weapons holstered around their hips.

"I assure you, officer," Hortense was saying, "only those with licenses possess a firearm. And we have no secret stash of explosives anywhere on our facility."

To Greg, Daphne texted: *Who are those men?*

The officer holding the leash said, "The footage viewed by our superiors indicates…"

"Sir, that footage is not proof," Arturo cut in. "Like I've been trying to explain, we are an *acting* company. Everyone here is an *actor.*"

Greg's message pinged back: *ATF officers.*

"The report from our superiors indicates that real bullets were fired," the officer with the paper said. "Whether they were fired by actors or circus clowns makes no difference. We need to perform a search, and you are hindering that search."

Hortense and Arturo exchanged glances.

Daphne texted: *Real officers?*

"This is private property," Arturo said again.

"I've been trying to serve you this warrant issued by a federal judge," the officer with the paper said.

I don't know, came Greg's reply. *If Giovanni hadn't been texting you a play by play, I'd say no.*

"You hold on to that," Hortense said.

"If you don't allow us to conduct our search, we will do so by force," the one holding the leash warned.

Daphne shifted to the very edge of the bed and held her breath, clutching her phone and staring at Joey's computer monitor. Hortense Gray had crossed her arms and was staring down at the sidewalk in an uncharacteristic way.

"Your timing couldn't be worse," Dr. Gray said to the officers.

"Oh, then maybe we should come back at a more convenient time," the one with the paper said.

"Yes," Hortense said. "When would you like to return?"

"That was sarcasm," the man with the leash said. "Either cooperate or be prepared for a federal invasion. We can easily call for back up, if you choose to resist."

At that moment, the sound of a helicopter played over Joey's speakers and all four people on the screen looked up. Only the dog held still.

That's our helicopter, Greg wrote. *That's Lee Reynolds in the cockpit.*

"Oh, no," Hortense said, her face showing the kind of fear Daphne had never seen in the doctor's features before. "Sirs, listen. We are in the middle of another scene. Your presence will only cause confusion and possibly endanger lives. I must beg you to come back tomorrow."

Daphne's attention was then drawn to another window, in which two figures ran from the main building up the sidewalk toward the jeeps. The camera angle was a longshot, but she recognized the runners: Stan and Cam. Stan carried his pistol. Whether it contained real bullets or not was impossible to tell.

When they reached the pool area, they took cover behind loungers. Daphne held her breath as Stan pointed his pistol toward the officers.

CHAPTER TWENTY-ONE

Mayhem

Just behind the officers, a voice cried out, "G'day!"

Where the hell did he come from? Greg texted.

The Australian! IDK! she replied.

Daphne was surprised to see Bill—backpack and all—as he hiked over the lip of the canyon and down the path toward the jeeps with a silly, friendly smile on his face. The helicopter hovered close above the facility in the bright blue morning sky, causing the Australian to shout over the sound of the propellers.

He cupped his hands to his mouth. "I'm looking for Daphne. Is she here?"

While the officers and doctors were turned toward the Australian, shots were fired from the helicopter—at what Daphne couldn't see.

The others must not know about the ATF officers! Greg wrote.

Then he added. *Oh crap.*

Daphne froze as her stomach dropped.

A few people who'd been walking in front of the main building took cover inside.

"Why is the helicopter pilot firing on the resort?" Joey muttered. "Is he a fed?"

"No," Daphne said. "That's Dr. Reynolds."

As the helicopter circled the facility, it scattered a flock of seagulls in all directions.

"It is?" Joey clicked on the window with the helicopter and zoomed in, so that they could just make out Lee's face, even though he wore headgear blocking part of their view. "Yeah. You're right. Who's he shooting at, and why?"

"I think he's acting in an exercise," Daphne said, dazed and unable to breathe or swallow. "I don't think he realizes those officers are federal agents."

Then, in a whirlwind of confusion, the officers opened fire on the helicopter and at the crouched figures of Stan and Cam. Hortense and Arturo were dragged back with them and their dog behind the jeeps. The Australian pulled out his gun and cowered behind a boulder on the canyon ridge.

"What the hell?" she heard him say in his Australian accent.

Greg texted, *Pray this isn't what it looks like.*

"Lee!" Hortense cried, looking up into the sky at the now floundering craft from where she ducked behind a jeep. To the officers, she shouted, "Hold your fire! Hold your fire!"

"Stay down and shut up!" one of them ordered.

Joey clicked on the window with Cam and Stan sprawled in a tangle of loungers by the pool. Both were covered in blood, and more blood was pooling onto the deck from their bodies.

"Cam!" Daphne screamed. "And Stan!" She jumped to her feet. "Oh, my God, Joey! Do you think this is real?"

"It looks real," he said. "How can it not be real?"

Daphne texted, *Tell me this isn't real!*

"Cam is shot," Joey said. He stood up and paced around the room. "We have to tell someone. Who can we call?"

Is that real blood? Greg texted.

You tell me! she replied.

"Who can we call?" Joey repeated.

"I don't know." Daphne's heart was caught in her throat. She couldn't breathe. The room was spinning. She fell on her bottom on the bed.

Then she watched in horror as the helicopter fell from the sky and struck the main building. Several people evacuated from the front and back of the building, as though they'd already been huddled in the doorways watching the gunfire. Within seconds of making contact, the helicopter erupted into a ball of fire.

Daphne dropped to her knees. "Emma!"

Greg's text echoed her: *Emma!*

Several of the windows on Joey's monitor went blank.

Daphne felt like she was waking up and seeing Kara's still blue body all over again.

"Oh my God! Oh my God!" she repeated.

"People are hurt!" Hortense cried from behind a jeep. "We need to help them! They could be trapped."

And for the first time since Daphne had met Doctor Hortense Gray, the stoic woman who never showed emotion, even during the most emotional times, broke into tears.

Daphne's own sobs bubbled from her throat, and tears streamed from her eyes.

A second helicopter emerged onto the screen on the clearing behind the pool and tennis courts.

Who's in that helicopter? Daphne texted Greg with shaky hands.

I don't recognize it, Greg replied.

Three people in black uniforms with a stretcher made their way toward the bleeding bodies of Daphne's friends sprawled on the deck at the pool. As one of the persons in uniform attended Cam's wounds, the other two lifted Stan into the stretcher and carried him to the chopper. Then they returned for Cam.

In another screen, Hortense and Arturo had their hands cuffed behind their backs. Bill had also been disarmed and cuffed. He kept protesting and asking what was going on, but the officers kept repeating, "We need your cooperation."

Another window with a wider angle showed Hortense, Arturo, and Bill being led across the complex by one of the officers toward the chopper. They climbed inside, and then the bird flew up and left the scope of the cameras.

Where are they going? Daphne texted.

I don't know. I'll call you as soon as I hear anything, Greg wrote.

In another screen, the main building was enveloped in flames, and the people who'd evacuated had run out to the boardwalk to get away from the smoke. The boardwalk was crowded with faces. Daphne searched them and thought she saw Dave's and Vince's among them, but she did not see Emma's.

Then the live stream went dead.

CHAPTER TWENTY-TWO

Aftermath

Daphne was sure it hadn't been real, especially since there had been no media coverage. Joey had searched every news channel and website available. There'd not been a single report. How could an incident like a helicopter crashing into a building off the coast of California not make national news? She was sure there was only one answer to that question: the deep pockets of Doctor Hortense Gray had kept what must have been a staged event quiet.

There was also the fact that Greg had stopped texting or returning Daphne's calls. He must have been told to break all contact with her once he'd learned the truth.

Plus, Mrs. Turner didn't seem to believe it was real either, when, after telling their own parents what they'd witnessed, Daphne and Joey had called Pamela over to explain what they'd seen.

She, too, couldn't believe it had been real.

"It must have been another exercise."

Those were her exact words.

There was no way to replay the live stream, and so Daphne and Joey hadn't been able to convince any of the adults of the magnitude of what they'd seen or why they desperately wanted to return to the island, so they could see firsthand what was going on over there.

Her father said they couldn't keep throwing hundreds of dollars away on flights. So Daphne felt like she had no closure. This made it easier to believe that the resort was still operating and that all the regulars were just fine.

Mrs. Turner had tried calling Dr. Gray and some of the hospitals in Ventura, just in case, but she received no information and, instead of becoming frantic, kept assuring Daphne it must have been an exercise.

Then, three days after Daphne and Joey had watched the event on the live stream, Mrs. Turner came over, pale and trembling, to tell them she'd received a call from a hospital in Ventura.

"He's gone," she said, looking as though she might collapse. "I still can't believe it. I just can't believe it."

"What? What happened? Are you sure?" Daphne narrowed her eyes. Could Mrs. Turner be lying to her?

Mrs. Turner's hands rushed to her face, palms spread wide with anxiety. "Please don't. Everyone I've talked to today has said the same thing: 'Am I sure?' and 'It can't be true.' I can't take it anymore. My son is dead! Do you hear me? My son is dead!"

Daphne's mom helped Mrs. Turner to a chair in the living room.

Daphne sat on the sofa, stunned. "Why didn't the hospital call you sooner?"

Even her parents and Joey hovered over her, silent and dazed, like they'd just gotten off the Tilt-a-Whirl carnival ride and were too dizzy to speak.

"They couldn't identify him until the coroner performed an autopsy." Mrs. Turner broke down into tears on the word *autopsy*. "They said they called as soon as they figured out who he was and who he belonged to. Apparently, they called Carl first, and when they couldn't get a hold of him, they found my number."

Daphne chewed on her lip and shook her head over and over as the tears spilled down her face. "I don't believe it. I just can't believe it. Why wouldn't Dr. Gray identify him?"

"I asked about all three of the doctors," Mrs. Turner said. "The hospital didn't know who I was talking about."

"What about Stan?" Daphne asked. "They must have been taken to the same hospital."

"I have no idea," Mrs. Turner said.

"This makes no sense." Daphne crossed her arms, trying to not to explode.

"Please honey," her mom said. "You're not making this any easier on Mrs. Turner.

"They're sending him home in the morning," Mrs. Turner added. "My favorite uncle came home in a box, after he was killed in Viet Nam. I never thought my son would come home the same way."

Daphne ran from the bathroom, where she was sick in the commode.

Cam's funeral was miserable for Daphne. Not only was her heart crushed into fragments that seemed to cut her from the inside out over the loss of Cam, but every time Brock touched her to try to comfort her, she only felt worse. His touch was painful. She wished she could curl into him and soak up his offers of love. She desperately wanted to reclaim his chest as that safe feeling of home. But she felt strange in his arms, as though he were a stranger, and her home was somewhere else.

And the fact that Cam's casket remained closed made it even more difficult for Daphne to say goodbye. She needed to see Cam's face one more time. She still couldn't believe he was gone. When she'd asked Mrs. Turner about it, the woman replied that it had been too long since his death. A closed casket had been strongly recommended by the funeral home.

So Daphne created a fantasy in her head where Cam was still alive. He was back on the island. Dr. Gray had said they would drive out the subscribers and then lay low. Then they would rebuild. Cam had to be alive, helping the doctor to reconstruct the Purgatorium.

She refused to believe he was gone.

This fantasy helped her to complete her G.E.D. when going back to school had been impossible for her emotionally. She supposed her parents had already gone through the GED process with Joey, and that had made it easier for Daphne to plead her case. Joey even helped Daphne get through it all.

Just when she thought she might be coming up for air, two things happened to pull her back under. First, Mrs. Turner announced that she was moving away to live closer to family. Her divorce from her husband was final, and now that Cam was gone, she needed to get away. As Daphne's only remaining link to Cam, other than the letter he had left her (which she read several times a day), Mrs. Turner had become a dear friend to Daphne. They had settled into a ritual of sharing coffee together each morning on Mrs. Turner's back patio, where they sat and watched the hummingbirds drink from the feeders hanging from the tree branches. They would reminisce, especially about the treehouse, where so many of Daphne's childhood adventures with Cam, Joey, and Kara, had taken place.

"You should go up there again," Mrs. Turner would say, almost every morning, but Daphne couldn't bare it.

The second thing that had pulled Daphne back under was an unexpected proposal from Brock. Things had been shaky and distant between them at best. Why would he propose? Maybe he thought things would improve between them if they were engaged.

He'd taken her to eat at the restaurant on the top of the Tower of Americas in downtown San Antonio. It was a revolving seafood restaurant with amazing views of the city and beyond. They'd eaten together there before, on Brock's eighteenth birthday, not long before Daphne had begun to feel guilty for being happy—not long before she'd dropped out of school and spiraled into the deep depression, where survivor's guilt and post-traumatic stress disorder began whispering ideas of suicide into her ear. Maybe he wanted to revisit what he saw as the happiest time in their relationship, just before her emotional fall. Maybe he thought going back would lift her up from the out-of-control, downward spiral she was floundering in now. He couldn't have known he was drowning her.

She had been taking measures to prevent him from knowing his suffocating effect on her. Not wanting him to be miserable, too, she had tried to pretend as best as she could. But when he proposed, she realized she couldn't go on pretending. She couldn't live this life that wasn't her life anymore.

"I know we said we'd wait until after college," he started, "but that doesn't mean we can't have a long engagement. So what do you say? Will you marry me?"

She looked at the ring in the box cupped in his hands and frowned. Whether it was a marquis or an oval, she couldn't tell. How many karats? She couldn't process. Tears sprang to her eyes and blurred her vision.

"It's too soon," he said. "I'm so sorry. I should have known." He closed the box and tucked it away in his pocket, and then leaned over and kissed her tear-stained cheek. "It's okay. Take your time. Take all the time you need."

He deserved someone else. Someone who could love him fully. Someone who was more than a halfling—for that's how she felt, no longer whole.

Halfling. That's what Cam used to call Kara. He used to call her Halfling and, less often, little Hobbit.

"Brock," she said through lips moist with her tears.

He closed his eyes and sighed. He knew what she wanted to say. She didn't even have to say it. She realized then that he'd known she was only pretending, and he'd been pretending not to know.

She went home and reread Cam's letter for the hundredth time, the hundredth-and-first, the hundredth-and-second, and again and again, until she finally fell asleep:

Hey Daphne,

Thanks for helping us. I'm sorry we didn't get to say goodbye.

I know you're probably back with Brock, but I want you to know that the days we shared together here on the island were the best of my life.

Yours Always,

Cam

P.S. Don't ever forget—No matter how you cook a Wookie steak, it always comes out Chewy.

P.S.S. If you ever do break up with Brock (I know, I'm just fantasizing here, but), go to my treehouse. I swear it's got rehabilitative qualities, especially if you follow your heart. You never know. Maybe one day it will lead you back to me.

CHAPTER TWENTY-THREE

Ghost Island

In July, Mrs. Turner moved out the last of her things and put the house on the market, leaving it in the hands of a real estate agent. Daphne was devastated, not only to lose her connection to Cam, but also to see the house so bare and vacant, an empty shell of a childhood haunt. She and Joey asked to walk through it one more time while the taxi at the curb in front waited to take Pamela to the airport.

It had been a mistake to walk through each room, because the memories of good times with both Cam and Kara hit her like an entourage of missiles, flying at her from all directions. She'd become accustomed to walking through her own home and not seeing Kara in every little thing; but this was something new. Both Kara and Cam seemed to be speaking to her from the dead.

Joey showed no emotion, but he was as white as a sheet. This was hard for him, too. She tried to hug him, but he stiffened.

They said goodbye to Pamela. Daphne wept as she held onto her. It was hard to let her go.

That night, her parents called her and Joey into the living room. They told Daphne how proud they were of her finishing her GED in spite of everything she'd been going through. They were happy that she had agreed to enroll for the upcoming fall semester at the same community college as Joey. They were also proud of Joey's 3.6 GPA. To celebrate these accomplishments, they wanted to go on a family vacation in August and wanted to know where Joey and Daphne would like to go.

"The sky's the limit," their dad said. "Greece? Rome? Hawaii?"

There was only one place Daphne wanted to go. When Joey said it before her, she busted out laughing and hugged his neck.

"Santa Cruz Island," he said again, when their parents stared dumbly back at them.

"Please, please, please!" Daphne begged.

In early August, all four of them flew across the southern states to Ventura, California and took the one-hour ferry ride to the island. Daphne was both ecstatic and apprehensive. Part of her felt strongly that Cam must still be alive and the Purgatorium under repair; but another part of her feared seeing the truth of its (and his) end with her own eyes.

Because her mother had refused to camp where there wasn't a fresh supply of drinking water and accessible toilets, they went ashore at Scorpion Anchorage, arriving at mid-morning, and set up camp in the valley at site number twelve—directly next to the one where Daphne had camped over spring break. As they pitched their tent beneath the hot sun, her eyes kept wandering over to site number thirteen, where Cam had kept her warm in her sleeping bag and had told her he loved her.

It seemed like yesterday.

As soon as they had finished, Daphne begged her parents to let them get started, but they were hungry and wanted to fix lunch before hiking the ten miles to Prisoners Harbor. They ate their sandwiches together at a picnic table. None of them seemed to enjoy themselves, though, and it wasn't because of the gluten-free bread they ate for Joey's sake. Her parents were apprehensive, too—she could tell—probably because they knew how she felt and were worried about how she would react when she saw for herself that the Purgatorium was no more.

Joey didn't seem so much apprehensive as curious. Although not eager, he was looking forward to seeing the grounds of the resort, so that he could piece together what had happened. When they had finished the last of their lunch, he seemed as happy as she was to strap on their minipacks of snacks and water and head toward the center of the island.

"I don't know what you expect to find," her mother said for what seemed like the hundredth time.

"This is a beautiful island," Daphne snapped. "Can we just try to enjoy it?"

Prisoners Harbor couldn't come soon enough.

It was a long hike beneath the hot summer sun. The hills were more difficult for Daphne's mother than anticipated. Daphne began to feel guilty for making her parents spend their family vacation on what would likely be a miserable experience all the way around.

They could have gone to Greece.

When, after three hours, they finally reached the gate leading onto the conservancy side of the island, the same guard greeted her again.

"Got a permit?" he asked them.

"Well, no," her father said, turning to Daphne.

"I've got this." Daphne lifted her wrist to reveal the silver chain bracelet she had received last summer, the one the guard had said would keep the conservancy officers from questioning her.

"Ah. That doesn't mean anything anymore," the guard said.

"You've got to be kidding me," Sharon said.

"No, ma'am. That resort burnt down, and the owner, Arturo Gomez, abandoned it *and* the conservancy."

"Any idea why?" Joey asked.

The guard rubbed his chin and frowned. "It seems he got into some trouble and had to shut down his operation. We haven't seen neither hide nor tail of him since last March."

"We'd really like to see the place for ourselves," Joey said. "Any chance of that?"

"I suppose you could become a friend of the conservancy with a $100—or more—donation," the guard said.

"A hundred bucks?" Daphne's dad complained.

"Or more," the guard repeated. "We take cash and checks. Make checks out to the Nature Conservancy, Santa Cruz Island."

Daphne gave her father the most pleading look she could make without being embarrassingly obvious. What was a hundred bucks when they'd already come so far? Luckily, he pulled out his checkbook before she had to actually say anything out loud.

Once they were through the gate, they ascended the steep hill onto the canyon ridge and followed the road for a half hour into the resort. In spite of the heat and the feelings of guilt from watching her mother's struggle, Daphne felt giddy with excitement when she recognized the tops of the cabanas coming into view. Her stomach did a flip-flop, and her heart raced like the little engine that could.

But once they reached the crest, Daphne's stomach dropped, and her heart seemed to stop beating altogether. The place below was in ruins. Although a few of the cabanas closest to the entrance were still standing, the main building was nothing but ash and rubble, and the units closest to it were half-burnt. The remnants of the helicopter that had crashed into the main building were scattered all over the grounds. Where the beautiful, aquarium-bottom swimming pool had been was now a mound of rocks and dirt. The tennis courts were still intact, but one of the nets was missing, and the other was torn in two, and they blew in the wind like two ragged white flags of surrender.

She clutched her heart and broke down in tears.

Again, like a broken record, her mother said, "I don't know what you were expecting to see, honey."

They hiked down the sidewalk to take a look around. They may as well, even though Daphne had already seen enough.

Holding back tears, Daphne went to the first unit and tried the door, expecting it to be locked, but it opened. She called out to the rest of the family, and they all came to have a look. This was the unit Daphne had stayed in during her first trip to the island. The furniture, including the two striped chairs and coffee table, was intact, though covered with dust and cobwebs, but the paintings had been removed from the walls, and the side table lamp was missing. She went to the kitchen and opened a drawer. The silverware was gone. Most of the dishes had also been removed. The refrigerator smelled foul when she opened it, so she closed it quickly. The sink did not turn on.

"It's a shame," her father said. "This was a beautiful place."

"I don't know what anyone was expecting by coming here," Daphne's mother said.

Daphne was about to turn to her and say something she'd probably regret when the sound of a jeep emerging from the canyon ridge made her gasp. She ran from the unit and looked up the hill. A jeep was making its way to the old clearing, and behind the wheel was Marty! Daphne ran up the cracked sidewalk to meet him.

"Oh, my God, Marty!" she cried. Although he was one of the subscribers who'd threatened Dr. Gray with blackmail, Daphne was happy to see any sign of the Purgatorium. Any at all! Her heart was pounding with the run and with the excitement of seeing him. "It's Daphne." She caught her breath as he parked in the clearing. "Do you remember me?"

"Of course, I do, young lady. How are you?" He opened the door and climbed out, glancing down the hill at the rest of her family, who stood gazing up at them with looks of confusion. "And what are you doing here?"

"I saw the place go down in flames on the live stream last spring," she said. "And I came back hoping that maybe it had all been an exercise."

"You and me both, girlfriend."

"You mean you don't know? You don't know if any of it was real or not?" she asked.

"Howdy!" her father called from below as he began making his way up the sidewalk. "Are you connected with this place?"

Daphne's brother and mom followed, and once they had reached the clearing, Daphne made the introductions.

"I live in the old Christy ranch house," Marty explained. "Ever since this place went up in smoke, I drive down every few days to haul what I can salvage back to my house."

"You live there?" Daphne asked. "Permanently?"

"Yep. I own it, and part of the land, too. I was renting, but a few months ago, the conservancy sold it to me at a pretty steep price. I suppose they needed the money after Arturo left."

"Do you know what happened?" Joey asked.

"I have my theories," he said. "But they're only theories."

"We'd love to hear them," Daphne said, trying not to sound too eager.

"Well, my goodness, young lady. I never get company. Why don't you all join me for some dinner?"

Daphne and her family exchanged glances. Her mother looked pleased. Daphne was desperate to go, even though she didn't completely trust Marty. She needed to learn as much as she could about the Purgatorium.

"That's awfully nice of you," Sharon said. "But we don't want to impose."

"Oh, it's no imposition." He flapped a hand at her, as if to say, "Don't worry about it." Then he added, "Like I said, I never get company anymore."

He opened the back door to the jeep for Daphne, Joey, and Sharon to squeeze into. Then Daphne's dad climbed in the passenger's side.

"About how many miles is it out to your place?" Joe made small talk as Marty started the engine.

"Seventeen. About a thirty-minute jeep ride," Marty said from behind the wheel.

"That's quite a ways," Sharon said.

"I'd be happy to drive you back to your campsite after dinner," Marty offered. "Or better yet, I'll take you back in my boat."

"That's so nice of you," Sharon said.

"Yes, thank you," Daphne added.

"You're lucky we ran into each other at the *beginning* of the month," Marty said. "I just returned yesterday from shopping at the mainland, so I have plenty of gas and groceries. Toward the *end* of the month, things get a bit bare around my place."

"Well, we don't want to eat all your food then," Joe said.

"Oh, I have plenty," Marty said, turning down into Central Valley. "And I can always make an extra trip into town. It's not a big deal, really."

They followed the road toward the base of Sierra Blanca and then up a hill, not far from Laguna Point. The memories of last summer washed over Daphne.

"So, what are some of your theories?" Joey asked.

"I find it interesting that there's been nothing in the paper or on the news about a federal ATF investigation," Marty said.

"That's what we thought, too," Daphne said.

"It could be that, once the place burned down, there was nothing to investigate," Marty said, "or it could be that there never were any ATF officers. That's what I think."

"You mean they might have been actors, right?" Joey asked.

"Right."

Marty followed the road down a hill into trees. The shade was a relief.

Then he added, "I called all the local hospitals in both Ventura and Los Angeles, and I got zero information. I also tried to track down Hortense and Arturo. None of the federal detention centers, or the local and federal district attorney offices had any answers for me."

"What do you think that means?" Joe asked.

"It means they were never arrested or charged with anything," Marty said. "But I still don't know if it was because none of it was ever real, or if it's because not enough evidence could be found to warrant an arrest." Then he asked, "So you all have no information? You've learned nothing about what happened?"

"Nothing," Daphne's father said.

Once they'd arrived at Christy Ranch, Daphne and Marty gave the others a tour of the bunkhouse and the bridge before driving back to the road and around the ravine to the ranch house—since Haunted Bridge was for pedestrian use only. They parked and went inside. Except for the extra paintings, lamps, and furniture, the place looked the same as when Daphne had last been there. She asked if she could show her parents and Joey the tunnel that went down to the ravine beneath Haunted Bridge.

As they toured the grounds, Marty told Daphne's parents and Joey the stories she already knew about the slave trader and her ghost. They walked out to the beach a few yards from the ranch house and admired the sun casting colors on the waves, which were gentle here.

Then they walked back toward the ranch house, where Daphne noticed an island fox beneath a scraggily tree. As she neared it, it froze but didn't move.

"Is that…"

"Mini-me," Marty said. "He hangs around for my scraps. Poor thing. I think he's as bored as I am now that the company has left us. We keep hoping that one day they will all show up again."

Daphne wished she could hold the little fox in her arms, like she had last summer.

"Hi there, little fella," she said.

He looked back at her with curiosity.

"Where's your boat?" Joe asked as he followed Marty back into the house.

"Kinyon Point. On the other side of the bunkhouse, maybe a half mile."

Marty made a salad and then grilled shrimp and chicken on his grill out back, and they all sat on the deck, watching the water and visiting with him as he cooked. He wouldn't let any of them lift a finger to help. He kept saying he enjoyed it.

He offered Daphne's parents each a glass of wine, and Daphne and Joey were given iced cold Cokes. It really helped to make the trip a little nicer to have these luxuries, especially after so much disappointment.

They spoke of trivial things, until, after Marty had served them and joined them at the table, he said, "Oh, but I did track down that orphan boy, Giovanni. It's what led me to believe the whole thing was staged."

"Giovanni?" Daphne's jaw dropped. "Oh my God! Did you talk to him?"

"As a matter of fact, I did—well, his parents wouldn't let me speak to *him*, but *they* answered my questions by telephone."

"What did they say?"

"They said they never reported Dr. Gray or the facility to the ATF."

CHAPTER TWENTY-FOUR

Follow Your Heart

To appease her mother, Daphne and her family stayed a few nights at a resort on Santa Barbara Beach before returning home to San Antonio. They'd gone shopping, to restaurants, and on a sunset cruise. Daphne enjoyed spending time with her family, even though most of the time her mind was somewhere else.

If Giovanni's parents had never contacted the ATF, who had been sending Daphne the texts and claiming to be Giovanni? She could see no reason why Giovanni would have made that all up. So who?

Marty had given her the number he'd tracked down for Giovanni's parents. One night after she and her family had returned from dining out, she curled up on the sofa in their hotel suite and finally got the nerve up to call it.

"Hello?"

"Is Giovanni there?"

"Who's calling?"

"Daphne. I'm a friend of his."

"Hold on."

A few minutes later, Giovanni's voice came on. "Daphne?"

"Oh, my gosh. I can't believe it's you!" she said into the phone. "How are you?"

"I'm good. How are you?"

"I'm okay. Just confused about what went down at the resort."

"You're lucky my mom didn't remember who you were," Giovanni said in a quieter voice. "Lots of people have been calling here, asking questions."

"Who?" She knew about Marty, but who else?

"I don't know. They won't tell me, but they said I'm not allowed to talk to anyone from there. They've even talked about changing this number. I guess *you're* alright. So, it's closed down now, right?"

"I guess so. We were just there. It's all burnt down."

"No shit. Wow. I can't believe it."

"It's weird, but I got a bunch of texts from someone claiming to be you while everything was happening."

"Really? That *is* weird."

"So, you never texted me? No once?"

"I wanted to, just to see how you were and to tell you I made it back okay, but I got arrested at Scorpion Anchorage and they took every-thing—even my phone."

"Who arrested you?"

"Park Rangers. They called me a runaway and a truant and said they were going to have to turn me in."

"Oh, no."

"No, I was glad. I needed help getting home."

They talked a while longer, updating one another on what they'd each been doing. Daphne didn't mention Cam's funeral. She didn't think she could go there emotionally and still speak on the phone. After they'd hung up, Daphne continued to be preoccupied with the question. Who had texted her?

The day they arrived home from the airport, they stepped out of the taxi with their luggage and saw a moving truck parked next door in front of the Turner's old house. Daphne's heart sank. After helping her parents unpack, she went into her backyard and climbed the tree where she liked to sit and think.

She wondered if the new people would leave Cam's treehouse or demolish it. After all her losses, she didn't think she could bear to climb up into this tree one day and see it gone. The idea took hold of her and brought her to the verge of panic. She needed to go to the treehouse one last time to say goodbye, just in case.

The new owners were still supervising the movers, going in and out the front door and the garage. She hoped they wouldn't notice her climbing the wooden fence separating their two back yards. She glanced to the back windows of the house and to the French doors and saw people moving around inside. They could come out any moment and find her trespassing. That wouldn't make the best first impression on her new neighbors. Maybe she should hop back over the fence and ask permission to sit in the treehouse. Surely, they would understand.

But what if they said no?

With her heart pounding, she continued up the tree and opened the hatch at the floor of the house before climbing inside. The treehouse floor, which was about five feet wide and seven feet long, was covered with dirt and dead leaves; otherwise, it remained in remarkable condition. Cam's stepfather, Fred, had built it many years ago. It had benches along three of the four walls and a built-in desk and stool along the fourth wall. A six-foot-high ceiling topped it off. When all four kids were really young, they played school with that desk and a chalk board they used to have in there. Then they played club house. Then spies. Then fugitives. Tears welled in Daphne's eyes as she pictured Kara and Cam and Joey all sitting on the benches in there with her, creating the next game.

Freud was right about one thing: Childhood play was indeed a pleasure. She missed those days. They'd gone by way too fast. Tears streamed down her cheeks, and she let them fall. No one was here to see her, so what did it matter? The treehouse used to be crowded when all four of them were in it together, but now she was all alone, and she felt like there were miles of emptiness between the walls. Where had those years of her childhood gone? Here she was about to enter college, and her sister and best friend were gone.

As she was imagining and reliving some of the fun they used to have together, Daphne noticed something white tacked onto the bulletin board above the desk. She had at first mistaken it for one of the baseball cards that had been there for as long as she could remember, but the faded outline of a heart made her look at it twice.

She took the paper and held it in her hands. It was a big heart, and in Cam's crude print were two words: *Wilderness Island.*

Her vision was blurred from her tears. She wiped her eyes with the back of her sleeve, blinked, and looked at the paper again. It was shaking now.

When had Cam put this here?

Go to my treehouse…follow your heart…it might lead you to me.

Was it a coincidence?

With the paper in hand, Daphne climbed from the treehouse and, as quickly as she could, hopped over the fence to her own yard. Then she ran into the house and to her room, to her laptop.

In the Google search bar, she typed *Wilderness Island.*

Exmouth Gulf, Western Australia. Privately owned. Untouched paradise. Approximately twenty-six miles from the coast of Western Australia on the eastern fringe of the Exmouth Gulf.

Was this a message from Cam?

Go to my treehouse…follow your heart…it might lead you to me.

Daphne screamed.

It was cold in early September when Daphne got off the plane in Learmonth, near the Northwest Cape of Western Australia. She had used her personal savings to purchase her flight after weeks of begging her parents. They didn't want to pay for more travel expenses on the heels of their family vacation, and so, if Daphne was going to go, she had to pay for it. She was just grateful that they'd allow her to go at all. She sent a quick text to her mom to let her know she had landed safely.

As she followed the signs for the airport exit, she thought that, as much as she loved her parents, she didn't mind being alone. This was something she had to do, or she wouldn't be able to move on with her life. The "what if" would drive her crazy. She might be on a wild goose chase, but it was one she had to make, or go crazy for the rest of her life. She was glad her mother wasn't with her this time saying, "I don't know what you expect to find."

Daphne knew what she expected to find, but she couldn't allow herself to completely believe she would find it. Otherwise, the disappointment would destroy her.

She asked a woman behind a help desk to point her to the shuttle that would take her the half-hour drive to Exmouth. Then she went to the platform to wait. Another thirty minutes or more passed before the shuttle arrived and she was on her way.

The views of the gulf were incredible as they drove along the coastline. There was one other woman in the back of the shuttle sleeping. The driver made a few efforts at small talk with Daphne, but she was too nervous to maintain a conversation. She kept telling herself that if she found nothing but an exotic resort at Wilderness Island, it was still an amazing adventure and totally worth all the money she had poured into it.

To distract herself, she rummaged in her bag for her poetry journal and pen. The ride was bumpy, but she was able to jot down a few lines:

On dragon flames, I bare my soul
My soul to you alone.
If you're there to receive me,
I'll soar to the greatest heights.
If, instead, my eyes deceive me,

I'll burn to the ground.
But one day—I know from experience—
I'll rise again from the ash,
And with my dragon flames
I'll soar at last.

It was lunchtime by the time she arrived at Exmouth, but she was much too nervous to stop and eat. She had the shuttle drop her off at the port to meet the ferry.

The ferry ride was another hour. Although the view of the glass-like gulf was breathtaking as it reflected the sun and sparkled like diamonds, Daphne was cold and scared.

"Dragon flames," she muttered beneath her trembling breath. "I've got dragon flames."

"Wh'dya say, mate?" the captain asked.

"Huh? Oh, nothing. Just talking to myself."

The captain grinned. "I do that all the time, mate."

When, at last, the ferry reached the island, there was no one around to meet her.

"Follow the path straight into the jungle," the captain said. "There will be a house at the end of it."

"Can you come back for me in an hour, in case I've come to the wrong place?" she asked.

"I don't normally come out here twice in one day, miss, but I suppose I could wait around and get some fishing in, if you pay me for my time."

"How much?"

"One hundred dollars."

She was relieved he hadn't asked for more, because she would have paid the remaining five hundred dollars in her wallet.

"It's a deal."

"I'll need half of it now, to stay."

She reached into her bag for her wallet and handed him a crisp fifty-dollar bill.

He gave her a nod of gratitude and helped her from the boat.

With her travel bag slung over one shoulder, she hiked along the path toward the center of the island. It was much different from Santa Cruz—much lusher and thicker with a great variety of plant life. Not far from the pier, rows of trees towered overhead in canopies that blotted out the sun in places. At least it wasn't as cold as it had been on the ride over, and there was less wind.

Thinking she should have asked the captain how long it would take her to reach the house on foot, she was surprised when she nearly tripped on the front stoop. It had been completely hidden by trees until she was standing right in front of it.

She stepped up onto the wooden deck and knocked on the door. She couldn't steady her hands from the nervous jolts of excitement and fear.

"Come in!" a man's voice called out in an Australian accent.

It reminded her of Bill.

She opened the door and stepped inside and nearly fell over with shock.

The man behind the desk in the front room *was* Bill.

He stood up at once. "Daphne? What a surprise. Does anyone else know you've come?"

"My parents. And my brother."

"But no one else? You didn't tell anyone else, did you?"

She shook her head. "So, you were with Dr. Gray all along?"

"She recruited me before we met, yes, but the others didn't know. She needed an island, and I needed an adventure. I was testing out the joint before making her any promises. I must say, I was rather pleased."

"This is *your* island?"

"I inherited it from my parents."

"And Dr. Gray…she's rebuilding the Purgatorium?"

"That's right."

"And Cam?" She swallowed hard, trying not to get her hopes up. "Please tell me Cam's alive." Tears rushed to her eyes.

CHAPTER TWENTY-FIVE

Living Art

Please, Bill," she said. "If you're here with Dr. Gray, then you must know if Cam is dead or alive."

Before the Australian could answer, the door flew open and hit against the interior wall. Daphne turned around and her knees buckled.

It was Cam!

"Daphne?"

He caught her in his arms. At first, she couldn't speak, couldn't breathe. Then her breaths came fast. She was hyperventilating.

"I can't believe you're here," he said. "I saw you from the hilltop, and I thought I was hallucinating!"

"I'll give you two some privacy," Bill said before leaving the room.

"Put your hands over your head," Cam said, lifting her arms to help her breathing go back to normal. "Oh, Daph! I'm so happy to see you!"

Once she caught her breath, Daphne asked, "How could you? How could you allow me to believe you were dead? And what about your poor mother?"

"My mom's here," he said.

Daphne's mouth fell open. "What? She knew?"

"Not until after the funeral," he said. "When I came home to tell her the truth, I saw you walking across your lawn to the front door with Brock, and I decided it was probably better if I just stayed gone."

She shook her head. "It was cruel. You're my best friend. Even if I *were* still with Brock, I'd want to know if you were alive or dead."

"*Were* still with Brock? Does that mean you *aren't* with Brock?"

"We broke up."

He took her in his arms. "I know you're angry and confused, but everything I did, I did for you."

"That's not how it feels."

She was so angry to have been tricked, and yet she was so relieved and full of joy. She was the happiest and the angriest she'd ever been in her life. Tears poured down her cheeks, and her bottom lip quivered uncontrollably. Emotions rushed through her system and made her dizzy and faint. Her stomach clenched, and she worried she might be sick.

"I need to sit down," she said.

He took her across the front room to a sitting area where there was a little sofa and coffee table with magazines fanned out on one corner.

"I need you to tell me what happened," she said. "Don't leave out a single detail. And then I want you to tell me why. First tell me about Stan, Emma, and Dr. Reynolds. Are they alive?"

Cam nodded. "And completely uninjured."

She let out the breath she'd been holding and slumped against the back of the couch.

Cam sat up on the sofa and faced her, taking one of her hands in his. "You knew the plan. Make the watchers flee. Right?"

She nodded.

"Well, we discovered that someone—probably Roger—had put a surveillance device in your backpack as you and Greg were leaving the island."

"Why couldn't I hear it on the live stream?"

"You had to click on the window to hear it. You and Greg just never clicked on it, probably because the video was just a gray smudge."

Daphne tried to remember if there had been a gray window in the lower part of the screen back at the hotel, but she couldn't recall.

"Anyway, we could hear everything you and Greg said, except when you were on the ferry and when you were in the taxi. Those parts were gurgled."

Daphne thought back to what she and Greg had talked about. Had they directly said anything about the plan to make the subscribers leave? Blood rushed to her face.

"They heard about Emma and everything," Cam said. "We were freaking out."

"Why didn't someone try to call us?" Daphne said.

"We all heard it at the same time. Calling you would achieve nothing. But then I had the idea of making it look like Giovanni was bringing the feds."

"It was *your* idea?"

He nodded. "So we sent Bridget out to send you a couple of texts claiming to be Giovanni."

"Bridget sent them?"

"Yeah. And thank God you bought it, because it gave the plan another fighting chance."

"But why make us think you were dead, Cam?" Tears tumbled down her cheeks, and her throat was suddenly tight. "Why make us go through your funeral?"

"Oh, Daphne." Tears welled in his own eyes as he leaned forward and pecked the tip of her nose with his lips. "The subscribers didn't just go away after the exercise. They tried to hunt me and Stan down in every hospital in every city of every country."

"Are you serious?"

"They called every police station, every federal prison, every federal agency, and so forth looking for Arturo and Hortense. Arturo finally met up with some of them and told them his side of the story—that the charges had been dropped.

"They were stalking your house, my mom's house, Stan's parents' house—everyone who had any connection to anyone affiliated with the Purgatorium."

"My house?"

"Absolutely. Hortense had gotten rid of Arturo…"

"How did she get rid of him? You don't mean…"

"Oh, my God, no! She'd never. No. She had this big scene where she confessed her love for Lee…"

"What happened to Lee? I saw him in the helicopter when it went up in flames. How did he make it out okay?"

"He jumped from a low altitude before the bird hit the main building. The whole stunt was planned. He was even wearing a protective helmet. Everyone had already been evacuated to the boardwalk."

"So, he's here?"

"Yeah. He's here. Everyone's here."

"And Lee and Hortense are…"

"I don't know. I can't tell."

Daphne frowned. "Why couldn't you call me? Why couldn't you tell me the truth?"

"We didn't want to risk it. If you accidentally said something that was overheard…"

"But a funeral?"

"Did you see Pete there? He actually went to my funeral. My mom recognized him. There were probably others there, too."

"It was all to convince the watchers."

"Stan and I waited until May. It was Mother's Day when we each went home incognito and revealed the truth to our parents. We made them promise to tell no one, just in case the subscribers hadn't yet given up."

"I can't believe you could tell your mom and not me." Daphne's tears started up again.

"I was going to. I really wanted to. But you and Brock looked so happy, and I didn't want to interfere with that. I really wanted you to be happy, even if it meant it wasn't with me."

"Oh, Cam."

"But also, I couldn't take the rejection all over again. I'd rather believe you would have chosen me had I lived."

"I would have chosen you. I did choose you."

He searched her eyes for confirmation, as though he couldn't believe what he was hearing. "That's when I had the idea of leaving you the clue in my treehouse. I thought that if you and Brock broke up, and if you really missed me and really loved me, you might go there. I thought if you didn't go there, then we weren't meant to be; but if you did, then the universe would lead you to me."

"Did your mom know about the clue?"

"Yes, but I made her swear on her mother's grave not to tell you. I didn't want you to find me unless it was because we were meant to be together."

She took a deep breath.

"Do you think you can forgive me?" he asked.

"I'm here, aren't I? I wouldn't have come unless I was hoping…"

Before she could finish her sentence, his lips were on hers hard and fierce and full of emotion. His hot tears fell on her cheeks. She kissed him back, unable to believe all that was happening—all that had happened. As incredulous as it all seemed, she cherished this moment, this absolutely brilliant moment that meant maybe, just maybe she would get her happily-ever-after after all.

In another moment, he stood up and pulled her into his arms and kissed her some more. Then he gave her a smile and asked, "How would you like a tour of the place?"

And she realized that if she was going to have her happily-ever-after, it would have to be here, at the Purgatorium. In spite of how scary that seemed, it was also exciting and thrilling. They would make living art together. She would become an artist of sorts. They would create stories together. They would help heal countless people who suffered, like she suffered, with depression and other problems. Without pressure from greedy subscribers, they could keep it safe. She was instantly infused with purpose and resolve. In that second, in that inviting look on Cam's face, she saw her future, and it felt amazing.

THE END

Thank you for reading my story. If you enjoyed it, please consider leaving a review. Reviews help other readers to find my books, which helps me.

Please enjoy this excerpt from a book in my *Nightmare Collection* called *The Mystery Man.*

First Day

Denise Walker ran in the hot sun across the Trinity University campus from Northrup Hall toward Chapman. The glare from the sun reflecting off the library windows and the metal sculptures and concrete sidewalk made her feel as though the universe had a spotlight on her.

It was hard to believe that a week ago, she'd held her father's gun to her temple and had come closer to going through with it than she'd ever come before.

When she reached her physics class and peeked inside, she groaned. Unlike the last class, this was an auditorium-style room with over fifty students. There was little chance she wouldn't be noticed. Biting her bottom lip, she slipped through the entrance as inconspicuously as possible to the nearest empty seat. When she looked up, the professor was staring at her.

He continued to stare, first with his eyes wide, and then narrowed, as if he recognized her. She wondered if she'd met him at student orientation or at the convocation, but she was sure she would have remembered him. He was young, attractive, well-built, and tall. His skin was dark, as was his short curly hair. Startling emerald eyes gazed at her from his baffled and beautiful face. How long would he continue to stare?

The blood had rushed to her cheeks, and she looked away, as she picked through her backpack for a notepad and pen.

Once she had unfolded the swivel desktop over her lap and had opened her notepad to the first page, Denise looked up to find the professor was still staring at her. She glanced around the room. Other students were now looking at her, too.

"I'm sorry I'm late, Professor Nadir," Denise said as she nervously twirled a strand of her black hair around her index finger. "I went to room 124 in Northrup Hall by accident and didn't realize I was in the wrong classroom until after the teacher had taken attendance."

The professor surprised her with a grin. He had an adorable face when he smiled, and this relaxed her. He muttered something beneath his breath—she wished she could hear it. Then he said, "That's perfectly fine, Dee—er, Denise."

What the heck? How did he already know her by name in a class of over fifty students?

"As I was saying," the professor said. "If you bought your textbook, return it. Get your money back. Everything in it is outdated." He paused and glanced at the students and then found Denise again. "What I'm about to teach you in this course will blow your mind."

Denise looked away, embarrassed again by his attention, and scratched out a note on her notepad: *Blow my mind.*

"The very first lesson I want you all to understand is this: Contrary to Einstein's theory, it *is* possible for an object to travel faster than the speed of light. It only appears to be otherwise, because the object traveling at this speed is *without* light, and therefore, *invisible.*"

Denise couldn't stop herself from raising a hand.

Professor Nadir laughed. Why would he laugh? But she kept her hand raised until he called her by name.

"If the object is invisible, how can your statement be proven?" she asked.

"Aha!" he said, smiling wider and lifting a finger in the air. "I'm glad you asked. That will be the topic of our first unit. Before tomorrow, I want you to read everything you can find on Einstein's theory of relativity. I'm releasing you early today, but don't get used to it. See you next time."

Denise glanced around at the other students gathering their backpacks and purses and folding their desks before making their way down the rows and out of the room. Brian Jameson stood at the top of the steps near one of the back exits. Brian Jameson? She hadn't noticed him among the crowd of students, and now her heart skipped a beat. His body had filled out—was more muscular than it had been in high school. His brown hair had grown out into wavy locks that fell to his ears. She waved at him and then turned away, down the steps toward the professor.

As Professor Nadir was packing his leather satchel, he didn't see her coming toward him. She cleared her throat. When he looked up at her, a huge smile crossed his face. It was perplexing and breathtaking.

"I want to apologize again for being late," she managed to say, despite how captivated she was by the man standing in front of her. "I was hoping to make a better impression on the first day."

"You have nothing to fear." He winked. "Consider me greatly impressed."

A chuckle escaped from her throat as blood rushed to her cheeks. "That hardly seems possible." She wondered if he was teasing her. "However, I'm very impressed by how quickly you learn your students' names."

Through his chocolate complexion came the pinkish hue of his own blush. "I'm not good with names. I called attendance, and it was only by the power of deduction that I came to know yours."

This was getting awkward. "I was the only student missing out of fifty or sixty?"

"Seventy-two. And there were seven missing, but you were the only female."

She felt relieved and gave him a nod of understanding. The tension left her body as she was reassured that nothing out of the ordinary was going on between them.

He swept up his book satchel and headed toward the front exit. "I'll see you on Wednesday, Denise."

"Have a good day, Professor," she said.

A whirlwind of heat washed over her as she watched him leave.

"Denise!"

She glanced up to the exit at the back of the room where Brian was waiting. So, he'd waited for her. As she raced up the steps, two at a time, she wondered what on earth he could possibly have to say to her. She met him on the landing, where he was holding the door open.

"That was strange," he said.

"I know. Right?" She stepped into the hallway, where others were headed to lecture halls and classrooms. "Long-time, no-see. How've you been?"

"Not as good as I am now," he said with a cheesy smile. "Are you going to another class?"

"Composition. You?"

"Calculus."

"How fun." Brian knew her well enough to know she wasn't being sarcastic. They both loved math.

"And after that?" he asked, as they rounded the corner of the hall-way.

"I have a break, for lunch."

"Want to meet up at Earl Abel's? Around eleven-thirty?"

She smiled up at him. "Okay. Yeah. Sure."

As they parted ways in front of her next classroom, she felt a tingle work down her spine. Brian was interested in her again, and she wasn't sure how she felt about it.

Earl Abel's was bustling with lunchtime diners and with the aromas of chicken, potatoes, and pie when Denise arrived and cased the entrance for Brian. When she didn't spot him, she stood with a crowd of others near the hostess station feeling unsure about her decision to lunch with him. Things had ended awkwardly between them in high school. Then she'd taken two years off to save money, and he'd gone on ahead of her to Trinity. They were the same age, but he must be a junior by now, and he hadn't so much as given her a text or a phone call in the two years since they'd last seen one another. Did he really think they could pick up where they'd left off?

The hostess, not much younger than she, asked for her name.

"Denise, party of two."

"I'll get you seated in about ten minutes," the hostess said.

"Thanks."

Maybe it *wasn't* Brian's intention to pick up where things were before, she scolded herself. They could be friends, couldn't they? This was just a lunch, not a romantic riverboat cruise or a sunset at Enchanted Rock. She closed her eyes as the wave of memories with Brian accosted her.

"Are you okay?"

She opened her eyes to see Brian looking down at her.

"Yeah. Fine. How was your calculus class?"

"Great. I have the same teacher I had last semester, for Calc Two. She knows her stuff. How was Composition?"

"The jury's still out on that." She lifted her brows and grimaced. "We shall see."

After a few more minutes of small talk, the hostess took them to their table and they ordered. Their food arrived, and they continued to chat. As Brian told her a little more about his major (math), his job (teaching assistant in the math department), and his aspirations (a professorship at a university after grad school), she continued to assess his intentions toward her. There was something about the way he gazed into her eyes that gave her the feeling he wanted to be more than friends.

She still didn't know how she felt about that.

When the check came, he offered to pay, but wouldn't that make it a date? Since she still wasn't sure what she wanted, she insisted on paying her share of the bill. Afterward, he walked her to her car and kissed her softly on the cheek.

"See you in Physics on Wednesday," he said in that low, gentle voice that used to send chills of pleasure down her body.

There may have been a few chills today.

"See you then, Brian."

That evening after her school day was over, Denise made a pot of beef stew and studied while it cooked. She did her calculus, biology, and composition homework first. Then, after she added the veggies to the stew, she sat at the kitchen table with her laptop and scoured the internet for all things related to Einstein's theories.

Only one article challenged the theory that nothing could surpass the speed of light, and it was written by Professor Nadir. Did the university know he was teaching students to disregard mainstream theories so that he could tout his own? She reached into her backpack and took out the heavy textbook, which the professor had said to return. Surely there was something valuable here. Denise wondered if she should drop Nadir's course and try to get into another. She was serious about her education and didn't want to waste time learning from some on-the-fringe scientist who could turn out to be a crackpot—especially one who distracted her with his amazing looks and intense eyes.

She decided to Google her professor. The results page was full of links:

"Chemotherapy Becomes a Thing of the Past, Thanks to Dr. Nadir," "Increased Brain Function with Light Therapy, by Markos Nadir,"

"Measuring Objects that Surpass the Speed of Light," and "The Future with Time Travel" were among them. Denise clicked on a few of the links and skimmed to see if they were about her professor. Every one of them referred to Markos Nadir as a Harvard professor. Was this a different man? She clicked on the Trinity University website and looked up his biography. There was that incredible face staring back at her again. According to his bio, he'd recently left Harvard to teach at Trinity. This was his first year.

Her curiosity was piqued. Why had he come to Trinity? And why had he reacted to her in his classroom as though he knew her?

When the stew was ready, she filled two bowls and carried them on a tray, along with glasses of iced tea, to her father's room.

His old console television was on, playing softly from on top of his antique chest of drawers, but he wasn't watching it. He was sitting in bed, staring at nothing.

"Hey, Daddy." Denise set the tray down on the bedside table and fell into her chair next to him. "Ready for some supper?"

"Mmm. Yes, Baby. Smells good. What is it?"

She handed him a bowl. "Beef stew. Does that sound good?"

"It sure does. Thank you."

"It's hot, so be careful."

She watched him blow on a spoonful. It always reminded her of the days when he blew on her food when she was a little girl. He puckered his thick lips, like a flautist. His long lashes shielded his dark brown eyes and touched his dark, hallow cheeks. His chin, covered in a salt and pepper scruffy beard, moved ever-so-slightly as he leaned closer to the spoon and slurped up the stew.

"Is it good?" she asked.

"Delicious, as always. Thank you, Baby."

No matter how thin he became, he always had a twinkle in his eyes for her.

"You're welcome, Daddy." She ate a bite. It was good. Each batch got better and better.

"How was your first day of school?" he asked.

"Interesting," she said.

"Why do I get the feeling that 'interesting' isn't a good thing?"

She told him what had happened in her physics class with Professor Nadir.

"Sounds like your professor was flirting with you," her father said.

"Daddy!"

"You don't seem to realize how beautiful you are—the spitting image of your mother."

"I'm more black than white. I take after you." Denise twirled a strand of her hair, coarse like her fathers, around her index finger.

"You have her bone structure and her almond-shaped eyes."

"Brown, like yours."

"True."

"I guess that makes me the perfect combination of you both."

"That it does! So, you better get used to all the attention you're going to get in college, from both the teachers and the students."

"Oh, Daddy. You're just biased."

"But not blind. Not yet, anyway."

She told him what Professor Nadir had said about invisible objects traveling faster than the speed of light.

"Now that right there sounds fascinating. Maybe you should invite him over for supper some time, so I can hear what he has to say."

"Oh, Daddy! I'm not going to invite my professor over for supper! That's not what people do!"

"Hmmm. We'll see about that."

The next morning, Denise sat in her chair in the room she rented at the salon, braiding extensions into her client's hair. The client, Lucinda, an old high school friend, sat on a bean bag on the floor between Denise's legs, watching Netflix on Denise's laptop. Netflix helped pass the time for her and her clients on Tuesdays and Thursdays (and sometimes on Saturdays), and it was the only chance Denise ever had to watch any shows.

When the final episode of their show ended, they dried their eyes, and Denise asked, "Now what do you want to watch?"

"I don't know," Lucinda said. "Maybe I need a break. I just want to sit here and close my eyes."

Denise thought she could use a little quiet time, too, so she braided in silence while her thoughts went back to the previous day—first to Brian, and then to Professor Nadir, who had visited her last night in her dreams.

It hadn't been an erotic dream, but it had come close and had been full of enough sexual tension to make her want to return to the dream as soon as she'd awakened.

Her thoughts were interrupted when Lucinda said, "Brian Jameson just tweeted that he had lunch with you yesterday." Lucinda turned to see Denise's face—for evidence, Denise supposed.

Denise couldn't suppress the smile. "It was just lunch, jeez."

"That's exactly how it started last time!" Lucinda laughed.

Denise pulled on Lucinda's hair. "Hold still."

"You can't change the subject. How was it?"

"The food was good."

"You know that's not what I mean."

"Brian's nice, smart, hot…"

"Don't you know it, girlfriend."

Denise frowned. "But I'm not sure I want to go there again."

"You were together our entire senior year, weren't you?" Lucinda asked.

"Yep."

"What happened?"

Denise shrugged, even though Lucinda couldn't see her. "I really don't know."

<u>CHAPTER TWO</u>

Second Week

Denise decided not to arrive early to her physics class on the following Monday, because when she'd done so the previous Wednesday and Friday, Brian had taken one of the empty seats beside her and had whispered to her throughout the lecture. He'd been funny and charming, as ever, but Denise didn't want to miss a single word Professor Nadir had to say. She'd become extremely interested in his discussion of space-time.

She walked through one of the back entrances at the top of the room with only a minute to spare. Brian waved from their usual seats—he'd saved hers. She waved back but indicated she was going to slip into one of the seats in back. He stood up, as if he would join her, but before he got very far, the professor began his lecture. Denise sighed with relief when Brian decided to stay put.

Denise's feelings of relief were quickly replaced with anxiety when Professor Nadir scoured the room for her face. She knew, before his eyes met hers, that he was searching for her. She wasn't sure how she knew it, but when his gaze fell on her, and he smiled and gave her a nod, she slid down in her seat, wishing to avoid the glances of the other students, who noticed.

Why did the professor seem to have taken an interest in her?

"Last time we discussed the nature of black holes," the professor began, "and how Einstein theorized they impacted space-time. We discussed gravitational lensing. Can anyone recall a good example of this?"

Several students raised their hands, and the one called on replied, "Einstein's Cross—a quasar in the Pegasus constellation."

"Yes," the professor said. "Thank you. You are probably wondering by now what black holes have to do with my claim that some objects are capable of moving faster than the speed of light. Well, let me explain. A black hole is a dense, dark mass that can only be detected by its impact on its environment. It's absent of light, yes?"

Denise and many other students nodded.

"It is the same with objects traveling faster than light," he explained. "They leave behind a shimmering effect."

Denise wrote *shimmering effect* on her notepad.

"From a distance, a fast-moving baseball appears smaller than one lobbed slowly up into the air, right?" the professor asked. "But the fast-moving baseball has greater mass than the slow-moving one, because the faster something moves, the greater its kinetic energy and, thus, its mass. Energy and mass are essentially two manifestations of the same thing. Do you follow me so far?"

Denise thought so.

"This increase in mass for the fast-moving object is the reason Einstein concluded that no object could travel faster than light," the professor continued. "He postulated that mass becomes infinite when it reaches light speed."

"But it doesn't?" Denise asked, before she realized the question had escaped her throat.

"No," he replied with a smile.

Brian glanced back at her and grinned.

"Everything is relative in the universe," the professor said. "Except the speed of light. It's the one constant."

Denise wrote, *The speed of light is the only constant in the universe.*

"And I don't believe dark objects travel faster than the speed of light in nature," the professor said. "At least, I have not seen any evidence of this. However, people are capable of manipulating objects through space-time beyond light speed. I have seen this with my own eyes. The shimmering effect."

Denise underlined *shimmering effect* in her notes.

As the professor spoke more about gravitational lensing and waving and the shimmering effect, Denise hung on his every word. She was one hundred percent absorbed and fascinated by the subject. She could hardly believe it when the class came to an end.

"Before I dismiss you, I want to remind you of something I have stated at the close of each class period. Can anyone guess it?"

A student raised his hand and said, "Time does not pass at the same rate for everyone. Time isn't constant."

"Precisely," the professor said. "I'll see you on Wednesday."

Denise raised her hand. "Wait, Professor?"

Markos Nadir smiled up at her. "Yes, Denise?"

"If time isn't constant..."

"Uh-huh?"

"And if light is measured in light-*years*..." she continued.

"A light-year is a unit of *distance*," he replied. "Not of *time*."

"But it's based on the amount of distance light travels in a year, and years are units of time."

"Very good, Denise," he said. "I knew you would be brilliant."

She lifted her brows as heat rushed to her face. What was that supposed to mean?

"As inhabitants of this planet," the professor continued, "we share the same frame of reference for what defines a year; thus, from our point of view, it remains constant."

The other students were showing signs of frustration and eagerness to leave the classroom—the professor had, after all, already ended class, and Denise was keeping them with her questions.

"Thank you, Professor," she said.

"The pleasure is mine. I'll see you all next time."

Brian caught up with her near the back exit and gave her a sheepish grin. "How's it going?"

"Good." She led him from the lecture hall, navigating through the crowd of other students.

"Did you do anything this weekend?" he asked, as he followed her through the hall.

"Just studied. You?"

"Same." Then he added, "So I was thinking maybe this weekend, we could, I don't know, do something."

Denise's throat tightened. She really wasn't sure she wanted to do this again. Everything about Brian still felt…unresolved. But, so as not to appear rude, she asked, "Like what?"

"Maybe dinner and a movie?"

So, he was definitely interested, and he was asking her out on a real date this time. Lunch was one thing. But dinner and a movie?

Before she could reply, he said, "Think about it, and I'll catch up with you later."

Friday night, after the movie, as she and Brian sat across from one another in a quiet corner booth at Olive Garden, Brian said, "So, why didn't you ever reply to my letter?"

She had just taken a bite of her ravioli, and it nearly fell from her mouth when her jaw dropped open. After she swallowed the bite, she asked, "What letter?"

He arched a brow. "What do you mean, 'what letter'? I poured my heart and soul out in that thing. You know what letter."

"No, I don't." Her heart seemed to stand still. "What did it say?"

"What? You never got it?"

She shook her head.

"Well, that explains a lot."

"Brian, what are you talking about?"

"I thought the reason we haven't spoken in the last two years had something to do with what I wrote in the letter," he explained.

Denise dropped her fork on her plate and was now numb and unable to eat. "What did the letter say?"

"That I adored you and wanted to spend my life with you."

Denise covered her mouth and stared at him in shock for nearly a full minute. "I don't know what to say. I had no idea."

"So why did you stop talking to me?" he asked.

"You stopped talking to me," she insisted. "You didn't return any of my texts or calls."

"You called me?"

"A gazillion times. I thought you were in an accident. I heard from a friend that you were okay. And then I saw you on Twitter and Facebook and figured you…"

"Oh, no," he said. "I dropped my phone." He snapped his fingers. "I couldn't get any of my contacts. I kept thinking you'd come by, like you always did."

His parents were never home, so they'd tended to hang out there more than they had at her house.

"Why didn't you come to my house?" she asked. "Or email me, or reach out to me on Twitter or Facebook?"

"I thought you read my letter and didn't feel the same way. I was scared."

"I wouldn't just stop talking to you," she said. "I'd never do something like that."

He looked down at his plate.

Denise wasn't sure how she felt about this news. Brian had written her a letter confessing his feelings for her and then had assumed she didn't reciprocate. *This* was what had happened? She was confused.

"I need a drink," he said suddenly.

"You want a glass of wine?"

"No, not here. It's too expensive. Why don't we go to Crazy Chuck's?"

Denise frowned. It was a club. She wasn't sure she was up for it, but Brian looked like he really wanted to go, and she felt bad for how things had ended.

"Alright," she finally said. "But I'm not twenty-one."

"Oh, that's right. Never mind, then."

"It's okay."

"Sure?"

She nodded.

They were quiet during the drive. Denise was still trying to process what Brian had said about the letter. He'd wanted to spend the rest of his life with her, and, when she hadn't come over, he'd assumed the letter had freaked her out. This changed everything.

She glanced sideways at him. But if he really had felt that way, he should have come to see her—or, he could have gotten her number from a mutual friend. He shouldn't have given up so easily. Maybe he was too young. Maybe if it had happened now, he would have tried harder and not run away.

Or maybe he was making the whole thing up, and there was no letter. She glanced at him again. Was he capable of being that deceptive?

Once inside the club, Brian left her standing near the dance floor to get their drinks. She was glad to have a little time away from him to think. She tried to remember all that had happened in the weeks when he hadn't returned any of her texts or calls.

The club was crowded with both college-aged students and people in their thirties. Men—young and older—stood along the perimeter of the dance floor near the two bars sipping drinks and watching the dancers— mostly women—perform a line dance. Some of them were boisterous and really into the dance moves, and others were tentative, still learning. Denise enjoyed this distraction from her confused feelings.

Suddenly a woman, tall and white, was beside her. Even her blouse and miniskirt were white. The only hint of color on the woman—about mid-twenties, Denise guessed—was the blue in her eyes.

"You see Hex, over there?" the woman said to Denise.

Denise followed the woman's gaze across the room, where a tall and older black man with rings on his fingers and one gold tooth smiled back at her before looking away. He was a hunk of a man—with more muscles than she'd ever seen up-close and personal. He was sexy in a bad way.

"Yeah?" Denise replied.

"He's not an easy catch—smart, wealthy. I've been trying to get him to fall in love with me for years."

"Maybe you should move on."

"Maybe I should." The woman laughed. "Well, he's into you, anyway."

Denise glanced at Hex again. He wasn't looking at her—was watching the dancers.

"I'm here with someone," Denise explained. "Excuse me."

She made her escape and sought Brian. He was still waiting in line to buy their drinks. She caught up to him and told him she was going to the ladies' room and would meet up with him after.

The line for the stalls in the bathroom was even longer than the one at the bar. Denise wished they hadn't come. She was tired and needed to pee.

She left the line in the ladies' room to return to the bar where Brian was waiting in line and was shocked to see another girl's arms wrapped around his neck. She watched them for a few moments, hoping to give Brian a chance. Maybe the other girl was coming on to him, and he was attempting to let her down easy.

But that's not what she saw. Brian leaned in and kissed the girl on the lips, then he whispered something in her ear before she nodded, smiling, as she turned to leave.

Denise had no time for this kind of nonsense in her life. If Brian didn't know what he wanted, then she didn't want to have anything to do with him. How dare he kiss another girl while on a date with her? What nerve? And what stupidity? Now things would be awkward in class for the rest of the semester.

Denise decided she would call a cab. She searched one up on her phone.

She avoided glancing in Brian's direction as she made her way through the crowd toward the exit. Before she reached it, the white girl caught up to her and said, "Hex wants to talk to you. Interested?"

Denise hesitated. She wouldn't mind using this opportunity to get back at Brian. Besides, what harm could there be in talking to the man?

"Where is he?" Denise asked.

"Outside, in the parking lot."

"I was just about to call a cab. If he wants to wait with me out front, I'll talk to him."

"You got it," the girl said. "He'll meet you there in a few."

Denise watched the white girl leave through the exit on her high stilettos, hips swinging. If that girl was so interested in Hex, why was she setting him up with Denise? She must not think very highly of herself.

Denise stepped out beneath the awning, where one of the club bouncers stood checking IDs. She took a few steps into the parking lot to get away from the line at the door. She had another shock when Professor Nadir approached her.

"You need to get out of here," he said. "Come with me, and I'll take you home."

"Professor Nadir? What are you doing here?"

He looked incredible in jeans and t-shirt.

"Saving you. Now come on."

Denise refused to follow him. "Saving me? From what?"

Markos Nadir moved nearer and whispered, "The woman in white and the man called Hex are setting you up."

His breath sent chills of pleasure across her skin, but she pulled back and studied his face. How did he know she'd been talking to the white woman?

"I've seen it before, at another club. I'm surprised they haven't been caught by now. Anyway, I noticed the girl talking to you and was worried you'd fall into their trap."

"I didn't see you inside."

"I haven't been in yet. I just arrived."

"I don't know what to say."

"Come with me. Or, at least, let me call you a cab."

She looked at her phone, which still displayed her search results for "taxi." Not wanting to wait around for Hex, the white girl, or Brian to come looking for her, she decided to go with Professor Nadir.

Besides, he was superhot in his faded jeans and snug t-shirt. Being alone with him made her hyper-aware of his every move, his every muscle. She liked that feeling.

In the car, she said, "Did you come alone or with friends?"

"Alone. I'm not from here."

"That's right. You're from Cambridge."

He gave her a surprised glance. "You looked me up."

"I was curious about you."

"Well, I'm not originally from Cambridge, either."

"Oh? Where are you from?"

He gave her another glance. "I was born in New York City, but that's not exactly where I'm from. You won't have heard of it."

She had a feeling he didn't want to talk about it, so she left it at that. "Where are we going?"

"To your house. I'll drop you off." Then he quickly added, "Which direction?"

"You're going the right way. I'll tell you when you need to exit."

She had a strange feeling that he already knew where to go.

When they reached her house, he pulled up beside the curb and stopped the car. "Listen, Denise. You're a smart girl, and I don't mean to meddle, but that Brian kid is not for you. And you should avoid talking to strange men at clubs. That's how women get hurt."

She was startled by his direct approach. What had felt like a sweet gesture by a knight in shining armor had quickly become a lecture from a righteous, judgmental dick.

"It sounds like you do mean to meddle, Professor." She opened the car door.

"I'm only trying to help."

"Thanks for the ride." She stepped out, onto the sidewalk.

"I'll see you in class."

She met his eyes once more before closing the car door and turning up the sidewalk to her house.

Her father was still awake, as usual, when she looked in on him. He didn't sleep much anymore—maybe four or five hours each night.

"Hi, Daddy," she said. "What are you watching?"

"Oh, hello, Baby. The History Channel. Nothing I haven't seen before. It's interesting, though. Did you have a good time with Brian?"

"Not really. I'm done with him, Daddy."

"Good. 'Cause I never liked him anyway."

They both laughed.

"I'm going to bed," she said. "Good night."

"Good night, Baby."

After she changed and crawled beneath her covers, Denise found herself thinking less about Brian and more about Markos Nadir.

EVA POHLER

Eva Pohler is a *USA Today* bestselling author of over thirty novels in multiple genres, including mysteries, thrillers, and young adult paranormal romance based on Greek mythology. Her books have been described as "addictive" and "sure to thrill"—*Kirkus Reviews*.

To learn more about Eva and her books, and to sign up to hear about new releases, and sales, please visit her website at www.evapohler.com.